Is Alcatraz
their ticket to the team?

The phone is dangling on the cord outside the apartment where Mrs. Caconi used to live. It's Scout, my best school buddy. He starts talking before I get the receiver to my ear. "I got us a chance. Bring your Alcatraz stuff to school today."

"What . . . why?"

"I ran into Beck. He's the captain. He doesn't believe you live there, but he's interested in Alcatraz."

I don't see how Alcatraz is going to get us on the high school baseball team. But if anyone can wangle a way on, it's Scout.

I pull the receiver away and give my ear a good scratch. "First we have to play better than they do. Doesn't this Beck guy want to see us play?"

"If we were sophomores, maybe . . . but freshmen? Not a chance. Look, I know you don't like trotting out your prison stuff, but could you please, this once?"

ALSO BY GENNIFER CHOLDENKO

GENNIFER CHOLDENKO

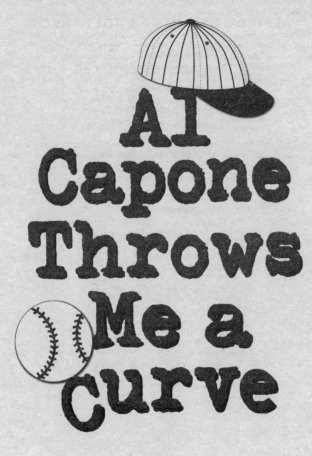

Al
Capone
Throws
Me a
Curve

A Yearling Book

This is a work of fiction. All incidents and dialogue, and all characters with the exception
of some well-known historical and public figures, are products of the author's imagination
and are not to be construed as real. Where real-life historical or public figures appear, the
situations, incidents, and dialogues concerning those persons are fictional and are not intended
to depict actual events or to change the fictional nature of the work. In all other respects, any
resemblance to persons living or dead is entirely coincidental.

Text copyright © 2018 by Gennifer Choldenko
Cover concept by Theresa Evangelista

All rights reserved. Published in the United States by Yearling, an imprint of
Random House Children's Books, a division of Penguin Random House LLC, New York.
Originally published in hardcover in the United States by Wendy Lamb Books,
an imprint of Random House Children's Books, New York, in 2018.

Yearling and the jumping horse design are registered trademarks
of Penguin Random House LLC.

Visit us on the Web! rhcbooks.com

Educators and librarians, for a variety of teaching tools, visit us at RHTeachersLibrarians.com

The Library of Congress has cataloged the hardcover edition of this work as follows:
Names: Choldenko, Gennifer, author.
Title: Al Capone throws me a curve / Gennifer Choldenko.
Description: First edition. | New York : Wendy Lamb Books, [2018] | Sequel to: Al Capone
does my homework. | Summary: Moose has his hands full during the summer of 1936
watching his autistic sister, Natalie, and the warden's daughter, Piper, and trying to get on a
baseball team by proving he knows Al Capone. | Identifiers: LCCN 2017026933 (print) |
LCCN 2017039456 (ebook) | ISBN 978-1-101-93815-7 (ebook) |
ISBN 978-1-101-93813-3 (trade) | ISBN 978-1-101-93814-0 (lib. bdg.) | Subjects: LCSH:
United States Penitentiary, Alcatraz Island, California—Juvenile fiction. | CYAC: United
States Penitentiary, Alcatraz Island, California—Fiction. | Alcatraz Island (Calif.)—History—
20th century—Fiction. | Autism—Fiction. | Brothers and sisters—Fiction.
Classification: LCC PZ7.C446265 (ebook) | LCC PZ7.C446265 As 2018 (print) | DDC
[Fic]—dc23

ISBN 978-1-101-93816-4 (pbk.)

Printed in the United States of America
10 9 8 7 6 5 4 3 2 1
First Yearling Edition 2019

Random House Children's Books supports the First Amendment
and celebrates the right to read.

To every kid who has a sibling with autism

Contents

INDUSTRY BUILDING
Capone and other cons do laundry here.

THE CELL HOUSE
Cons live here.

A GUARD TOWER
With crapper and privacy curtain

REC YARD
Cons play baseball here.

PARADE GROUNDS
Best place to play baseball

PIPER'S HOUSE
Fastball works here.

BACK ENTRANCE TO CELL HOUSE
Food deliveries arrive here.

BACK STAIRWELL TO WARDEN'S HOUSE

OFFICERS' CLUB

APT #2E
I live here.

APT #2G
The Mattamans'

THE CANTEEN
Bea Trixle, Jimmy, and
Piper work here.

METAL DETECTOR
Everyone entering
the island must
pass through this.

THE DOCK
Cons work
here.

APT #3H
Annie's

APT #3G
The Trixles' and Bea's hair salon

ALCATRAZ ISLAND (1936)

1. Potty-Training a Snake

································

Tuesday, May 26, 1936

Even when you live on a prison island with crafty criminals plotting ways to knock you off, summer is the best time of the year.

No tests. No homework. No getting up early to catch the ferry. No teachers who think you flunked a few grades because you're kind of big for thirteen and a half.

Summer is freedom. Not for the prisoners, of course. But for us kids who live on Alcatraz Island.

Naturally, summer on Alcatraz isn't like summer other places. For one thing, the weather in the San Francisco Bay can be colder and foggier than in winter. For another, kids can't go many places on the island. We're not allowed in the cell house, in the industry buildings, in the west-side gardens, on most of the beaches, and in all the guard towers.

Our fathers work in the prison up top, so they're allowed everywhere. But even with restricted access, there are two decent spots to play baseball: the parade grounds and down by the dock. And there's one other Alcatraz kid who can really play.

She's a girl. But still.

Baseball . . . that's what I'm thinking about as I shovel in my breakfast toast, hoping the last five days of school will go fast.

My father frowns at me, crushing crumbs with his fork. "Saw the warden at shooting practice this morning. He wants to talk to you."

I stop chewing. "The warden? Why?"

He shrugs.

"Uh-oh! Uh-oh!" my older sister, Natalie, mutters. Her blond-brown head is bent forward as she counts toothpicks in rows. She's tall, like my mom and me, but she holds herself in a way that makes her look younger and smaller than she is.

My father's hand hovers over Natalie's toothpicks. "Okay if I take one?"

Natalie hands him the last one in line.

We moved up here from Santa Monica a year and a half ago so Nat could go to a school called the Esther P. Marinoff, which helps kids whose brains aren't wired like everyone else's. My parents sacrificed a lot for her to go to that school. We all did.

My father was an electrician in Santa Monica, but he had a hard time finding a job up here. It's almost impossible to get work on account of the Depression. I don't understand exactly what the Depression is except it has to do with the banks collapsing and people not having money. The only job my father could get was as a guard and an electrician in the prison. Everybody likes him here, though, so he was promoted to assistant warden.

Since Nat's been at the Esther P. Marinoff, she's learned how to have a conversation—not just echo what you say. She still has a difficult time looking people in the eye, but she has been trying really hard. Now we're helping her make friends.

My father watches Nat move on to a new project: cutting pictures out of magazines and pasting them to boards. My mom has written "happy" on one board. Natalie hunts for pictures of people who are happy. There's another board for "sad," but Nat doesn't care much about that one.

"Look at you, sweet pea. One day you'll find a nice man to marry, and you'll live in your very own house."

My mother doesn't like when my father talks about Nat getting married. She thinks it's more than Natalie will ever manage, but my father says nonsense, his girl can do anything.

Dad strokes his bald spot. "You'll never guess who I drove up top last night."

I don't have to guess. I know. "Piper."

Piper is the warden's thirteen-year-old daughter. When I first moved to the island and I was stupid as a stone, I had a crush on her. Now I know better. I hope I do, anyway. Sometimes I get a little turned around by how cute she is.

Piper has a good side . . . but it's tiny and not easy to locate. Dealing with her is like potty-training a snake. Which end does the business? I don't even know.

I take a bite of a crispy corner of my toast. "Am I supposed to go before school?"

"Shouldn't take long." My father glances at the clock. "The warden's a busy man. And you, sweet pea." He turns to Natalie. "Happy day-before-your-birthday."

Nat doesn't answer.

Things have always been screwy around Natalie's birthday.

Every year Mom pretends Natalie is turning ten again, instead of fourteen, fifteen, sixteen, or, this year, seventeen. Mom wants Nat to be younger so she has more time to catch up with the other kids.

After breakfast, I put on my scratchy shirt and tie, my good trousers and squeaky shoes.

When my mom sees me, she takes a step back. "Moose! What happened to you?"

I shrug. No sense in getting her worked up. If my dad hasn't told her, I'm certainly not going to.

Outside, I trudge past the guard tower, which is a tiny room on three-story-tall metal legs. All the firepower on the island is up in the towers and in the gun galleries. An armed guard down with the convicts can be jumped, ambushed, taken down. But when a guard is up high with his gun trained on us, we're all safe. Or as safe as we can be on a twelve-acre rock with kidnappers, con men, hit men, bank robbers, criminals, crooks, murderers, and maybe an assassin or two.

I walk up the steep switchback to the top of the island, which really stinks. Alcatraz is the world's biggest bird toilet; plus there are three hundred and fifty prisoner toilets up here. They don't help the aroma, that's for sure.

The sky directly over the island is a crisp blue, but the fog is rolling through the Golden Gate. Blink once, it's sunny; blink twice and the world has gone gray.

I'm in no hurry to see the warden, so I take a detour by the recreation-yard wall.

My dad says the prison yard is a little piece of hell. Things happen there you don't ever want to know about.

The prisoners play baseball here on weekend afternoons. I've never seen them play, but I've heard them. One of the cons, a guy named Fastball, who works in the warden's house, made it to the minor leagues before his bank-robbing career got in the way. Another, Fat Fogarty, hits so hard, he's broken two bats.

It's scary that they give baseball bats to felons, but I guess baseball can make any guy behave. My father says baseball is as important inside the prison as it is outside it. He says the prison-game scores get posted right next to the major league scores on the menu every week.

I keep walking past the cell house, where a con is shouting about a hanging tree. I've never been inside the main part of the cell house, and I sure don't want to go in there, either.

Since a convict stabbed my father a few months ago, I haven't thought it was so great to live on an island with a bunch of murderers . . . especially with a sister like Natalie.

I don't think Dad understands that. He says I should have a positive attitude and not worry so much. But after your father almost dies, you don't look at stuff the same way anymore.

I scoot to the other side of the narrow road. I'd just as soon keep my distance.

When I get to the warden's mansion, I walk up the stairs to the stoop. From here you can see across the bay to San Francisco. I take a deep breath and press the doorbell.

A man in a white shirt, a black tie, and khaki pants opens the door. He's short, with hair like the fur on a stuffed animal. He has large brown eyes, an egg-shaped head, and a kind smile.

My father told me that "pass men"—men who work in the warden's house—are chosen from a small group of prisoners who are almost done with their sentences. Lifers—prisoners who won't ever go free—don't have an incentive to do the right thing. But dangle freedom in front of a guy and he isn't likely to cause trouble.

That's the theory, anyway. But I don't buy it, because last year the warden's pass men took me, Natalie, and Piper hostage. Those guys are in isolation now. I don't know how long they'll stay there. I hope forever.

"How's it going, Moose?" Fastball asks.

Of course Fastball knows my name. The convicts know my sister's favorite cake (lemon) and my father's favorite book (*Leaves of Grass*). Last year Dad forgot Mom's birthday, and a convict reminded him.

The prison yard knows everything.

They know more about us than we know about them. In most cases, I can tell you a convict's prison name, but not his real name.

There's Fang, who bit off a man's finger for refusing to hand over his wallet, Wrong Way Willy, a jewel thief, who got caught because he put the getaway car in reverse instead of drive, and Tommy Twelve, who killed eleven of his wives. The twelfth one comes to visit every month or so.

Fastball doesn't stick out his hand for me to shake. Prisoners aren't allowed to touch us. They'll get written up for that.

"Hey," Fastball says. "I heard you and Jimmy got a new game going."

I nod. "Escape from Alcatraz."

Theresa, Annie, Jimmy, and me pasted a map of Alcatraz to an old game board. Then we made steps that lead all around the island. Whoever gets on the ferry first wins. The cards you pick from the deck say things like *Wash extra laundry. Go forward 1 space.* Or *Get caught with a shiv* (a prison-made knife). *Go back 3 spaces.*

When Jimmy and I play, I always get to be Al Capone, Chicago's prized bad boy and the king of crime, who just happens to be in prison here. My game piece is a little cardboard gangster hat. Jimmy is Count Lustig, a con man and a counterfeiter. We have a tiny fake hundred-dollar bill for him. Then there's Machine Gun Kelly, who's a miniature machine gun, and Fastball, a tiny baseball.

Fastball grins. "I'd like to see it. Know some guys might be interested."

"Probably good to get some expert advice." I try to keep a straight face.

"Yup . . . got plenty of that. I understand you got yourself some business with the big man. Good luck with that." He moves out of the doorway so I can walk by.

The warden's house is full of fancy furniture that looks too nice to sit on. My feet sink into the runner carpet as I climb the stairwell. My stomach is mixed up, like it can't decide if I ate too much or I'm hungry.

Outside the door of the warden's library, the chandelier flickers, and classical music plays low in the background. My mother is a music teacher. She would know this piece, but I'm tone deaf and completely lacking in musical ability.

When I was eight, she asked me not to play in her recital. She said I was bad advertising. Now she tells me it's painful to hear me hum.

My eyes scan the hall to the closed door to Piper's room. Is she in there?

"Come in," the warden booms.

How'd he know I was standing here? The man's got good ears.

The warden sits up straight as a fishing pole in his deep-blue suit. Long gray hairs curl out of his eyebrows like tentacles.

His big desk, dusty law books, drawn curtains, fountain pen, and squeaky chair all look the same as the last time I was here.

"Close the door," he barks.

"Yes, sir," I say.

Should I sit or stand? Stand. Then I can make a fast getaway.

The warden gives me a once-over with his arctic-blue eyes. "I'll get right to the point, Moose. That unfortunate business earlier this year with Piper." He clears his throat. "You handled it very well."

It's been four months since Piper got mixed up in the counterfeiting operation with Count Lustig and was sent away to boarding school. Why would the warden call me in to tell me this now?

"Thank you, sir," I say.

"I'm concerned about her on the island this summer."

"She's going to be babysitting, right?"

His chair squeaks. He rubs his neck.

I heard he had to pay cash to the stores where she bought things with fake bills. They said she was supposed to earn the money to pay him back.

The warden leans forward. "I'd like you to keep an eye on her."

Being singled out to help Piper is like being the turkey picked for Thanksgiving. I dry-swallow. "Sir, um, I was, uh . . . How about Jimmy?"

I feel bad suggesting Jimmy, my best buddy on the island. He's not going to want Piper around any more than I do.

The warden fixes his eyes on me. "She doesn't respect Jimmy the way she respects you."

Respect? She doesn't respect me. She manipulates me.

He lowers his voice until it's gruff and gravelly. "I know she's a handful."

Am I supposed to agree with the warden that his daughter is a handful?

"Yes, sir," I mutter, my face hot. Then I stand up straight, locking my knees. "I'm sorry, sir, but I'm going to be in the city this summer."

"Doing what?"

"Playing baseball."

"All day? Not even the pros play all day, Moose."

I chomp on the inside of my cheek. "I'm trying out for the high school team. It's practically impossible to get on as a freshman. I'm going to have to work really hard, and besides that, I have responsibilities around Natalie."

"Piper can help you with her."

Piper? At best, Piper tolerates Natalie, and that's if I'm standing right there. I've seen her be so mean it was all I could do not to punch her.

"I don't think Piper is cut out for that, sir. I really wish I could help, but—"

He peers at me. "I wouldn't ask this of just anyone. But I know you, Moose. I've seen how thoughtful you are."

My cheeks flush.

He picks up a shiny, sharp letter opener and begins slicing open envelopes. *Zrip, zreep, zrip*—the paper tears along the crease. "If you have a problem, remember, my door is always open."

I stand there, dumb as a piece of meat.

He looks up at me. "I'm counting on you, Moose. I hope you know that."

My head nods like a traitor.

It's only when the door closes behind me that I realize I've just given my summer away like it wasn't worth two pennies to me. The warden is my dad's boss. I have to do what he says.

But, nobody can keep an eye on Piper. Nobody.

2. THE DOORMAT RULE

■■■■■■■■■■■■■■■■■■■■■■■■■■■■■■■■■

Tuesday, May 26, 1936

When I get off the ferry after school, the water is green, like unwashed teeth, and a wall of wind hits me. I hold my cap on, breathing in the smell of the dock: rotting wood and old fish. A seal barks in the distance. I look for his black head in the tossing, turning bay.

I'm headed for the steps of 64 Building when I see my Alcatraz friends—Annie Bomini and Jimmy and Theresa Mattaman—coming down. We all live in 64 on account of our fathers are guards, or, in my dad's case, the assistant warden. Annie and Jimmy are thirteen and fourteen. Theresa, Jimmy's little sister, is eight. Theresa and Jimmy look alike: short, with moon-pale skin; thick, black curly hair; knobby knees; and knobby elbows. Annie is pale, too, but she's taller than they are, with white-blond hair and large blue eyes.

Theresa still has on her school uniform. Jimmy changes out of his on the ferry home every day. Annie is all dressed up, and she's carrying a suitcase.

I pick it up for her. "Hey . . . where are you going?" I ask.

"Girl Scout camp."

"Now? School isn't even out yet," I say as a steamer disappears behind the big green mountain of Angel Island.

"They gave her permission to leave early," Jimmy says.

Annie, Jimmy, and Theresa go to Catholic school. They all get straight As. But Annie's the only kid who spends her free time in religion class. The nuns adore her. They'd give her permission to go to Mars if she asked.

"My aunt runs the camp. I have to help her get the cabins ready before the Girl Scouts arrive," Annie says.

"How long will you be gone?" I ask.

"All summer."

"All summer!" I drop the suitcase on my toe. "You're kidding."

Who will I play baseball with if Annie's gone? I'll miss her for all kinds of reasons, but that one bites deep.

The wind lifts Annie's hat off. She looks so grown-up in her traveling clothes: a jacket, a skirt, and small heels.

I chase down the hat and hand it back. "How come I didn't know that?" I ask her.

She shrugs, but we both know why. It's been awkward since we broke up. Having Annie as my girlfriend sounded like a good idea, the way eating an entire pie sounds like a good idea, but then, when you do it, your stomach hurts and you regret it.

We live so close to each other. We were always together. I adore Annie, but I didn't want to spend every waking minute with her. And when I told her that, I hurt her feelings. I didn't know being somebody's boyfriend would be so complicated.

"She's going to leave us all alone with Piper and the escaped convict," Theresa says.

Jimmy rolls his eyes. "How many times do I have to tell you? There's no escaped convict."

"Then who scratched at our door?"

"Maybe the wind blew against it. Look, they do counts every hour. They'd know if a guy was missing," Jimmy tells her.

"They could have counted wrong. I've counted wrong before. The only person who doesn't count wrong is Natalie," Theresa insists.

"Maybe it was Natalie knocking on your door," I suggest.

Natalie is the most predictable unpredictable person you'll ever meet. Usually she does everything in exactly the same way, unless something goes haywire, and then who knows what she'll do. She's been known to wander.

Theresa folds her arms. "If it was Natalie, she'd have come in."

Jimmy wags his head. "You've got a point there," he says.

Annie slips off her left shoe and massages her stocking toe. "What exactly did you hear?"

"It was a scraping sound ... *screep-screep*." Theresa does her best imitation.

"Could have been a gull," Annie suggests.

Theresa shakes her head. "Gulls don't sound like that."

"Neither do escaped prisoners," I tell her. "They want to get off the island, not come in for your mom's blueberry pie."

"Maybe they wanted a hostage." Theresa juts her chin at me.

"Excuse me, excuse me"—I pretend to knock on a door—"could I bother you folks for a little hostage, here?"

Annie and Jimmy laugh. Theresa doesn't. She's just winding up for a big Theresa-style grousing when Mr. Bomini comes out of the dock office, rolling his hand like he's spooling yarn around it. We know that means "hurry up."

Theresa snaps her mouth shut.

"Annie, really, do you have to go now? I was thinking we'd play ball today." My voice comes out more pleading than I would have liked.

"Let's see." She rests her chin on her hands, tapping her fingers against her cheek. "Do I want to spend all summer watching murderers unload laundry in the fog, or swimming in the warm sun?"

"But, Annie . . ." Theresa's shoulders drop low. "You don't want to leave *us*."

"Yes, she does. She wants to leave us," I say.

"I want to leave them"—Annie points at Jimmy and me—"but not you." Annie gives Theresa a hug.

Jimmy grins and bats Annie on the arm.

What am I supposed to do? Are there rules for saying goodbye to girls who used to be your girlfriend?

"Don't run over any Girl Scouts or anything." I lean in to hug Annie, but she blocks me with her hand, her face as red as a nautical light.

I stumble forward, shaking three of her fingers.

Mr. Bomini picks up Annie's suitcase. "You're leaving some mighty long faces. And one pair of extra-large feet." He looks down at my pups. "But they'll all be here when you get back. And the feet may be even larger." Mr. Bomini hits his palm to his forehead. "That's a scary thought."

I don't laugh. I'm still recovering from the hug attempt.

Annie follows her dad onto the boat, walking with surprising ease in her good shoes.

The bay is choppy and churned up. I hope it will be too rough for the ferry to go, but no such luck.

We stand silently, watching Annie leave. It feels like somebody died.

It takes me a minute to notice Theresa yanking my sleeve. "Moose? Moose? What were you doing at the warden's this morning?"

Why is it that nobody knows Annie's business and everyone knows mine? They can smell if my mom burns dinner. They can tell my mood by how I close my front door. They know when I have to wear dirty socks because we forgot to put our laundry bag out.

"Theresa!" Jimmy barks.

"What?" Theresa's hands fly to her hips. "I wasn't going to talk about when his dad almost got killed. I *wasn't*."

Jimmy's face flushes. "I know, but it's none of your business what Moose was doing at the warden's."

"It's okay." I shrug. "He sent for me. He wants me to keep an eye on Piper."

Theresa nods solemnly. "Well, that's good!"

"No, it's not. Who wants to spend the summer doing that?" I ask.

"Somebody has to do it," Theresa says.

When Piper got in trouble for the counterfeiting scheme, Theresa was working for her. Theresa didn't know the money Piper gave her wasn't real, and she hasn't forgiven herself for not figuring it out. We tried to tell her we didn't know either, but it didn't help.

Now Theresa believes Piper is responsible for every bad thing that happens anywhere. The dust storms in Oklahoma, the soup lines in San Francisco, and that crazy Hitler guy in

Germany who doesn't want Jewish people to compete in the Olympics. That's all Piper, too.

"I know!" Theresa's finger pops up like a struck match. "I'll help. I'll check her room every day for clues. I'll bet she knows all about the escaped prisoner."

"Breaking in to the warden's house . . . does that sound like a good idea to you?" Jimmy asks.

"I have to." Theresa stamps her foot. "This is serious. Remember that time she lied and almost got our dads fired? Remember when she dropped her purse on Mrs. Capone's toe? Remember when she sold the convict laundry service to kids at school, and *we* got in trouble for it? And that was before the fake-money stuff."

"We remember . . . okay, Theresa?" Jimmy says.

"Yeah, well, we got to watch her. We do." Spit comes flying out of her mouth.

Mrs. Mattaman leans over the second-floor railing of 64. She's standing with my mom, who's wearing a summer dress.

"Theresa! I need you—Helen and I are going to the Officers' Club. You come on up with us," her mom shouts down. Mrs. Mattaman always seems to appear when Theresa is driving Jimmy crazy.

"Okay, but you can't break into the warden's house," Jimmy says in a low voice.

"Oh, all right." Theresa's shoulders droop, and she drags herself up the stairs.

My mom says something to Mrs. Mattaman, and they both laugh.

"Your mom sure looks happy," Jimmy observes.

"She does." I agree. "Hey, you want to play baseball?"

Jimmy hates baseball, so he'll probably say no, but it's worth a try.

His eyes inspect his shoelaces like they're suddenly very interesting. "How about we play Escape from Alcatraz?"

I swallow hard.

It's difficult to imagine how anyone could prefer a board game to baseball. "Hey, guess what? Fastball asked to see it."

"Nice." Jimmy grins. "Think we'll get in trouble for showing him?"

"I'm supposed to be up there watching Piper. No harm in playing a game with her, right?"

"Right," Jimmy says as we take the stairs to the Mattamans' and grab the game. We're on the way up the hill with the board and the pieces in a flour bag when we see Piper coming down.

Her dark hair is shorter and her face is more filled out than I remember. Her lips are puffy and curvy and . . . okay, her lips are perfect.

Piper lifts a hand to keep her hair from blowing in her face. Her other hand is on her skirt so it doesn't fly up. "Where are you going?"

"Come with us. We're going to show Fastball our game. Besides, I'm supposed to be keeping an eye on you."

She groans. "Oh great . . . my very own policeman."

"More like a bodyguard," I say.

"That's better." She smiles. "Hey, I wrote you a letter from boarding school."

"I didn't get it."

"I know. I didn't send it. Want to see?" She pulls a letter out of her pocket and hands it to me.

Dear Moose,

You wouldn't believe how boring this place
is. The girl down the hall got excited when she
found a pair of underwear she hadn't sewn her
name in yet. Really, that's what people do for fun
around here. Sit around sewing their names in
stuff.

Every morning we stand up and say the rules.
There are even rules for how you say the rules.

And my roommate is full of herself. She farts
in her sleep. She burps in my face. She sleeps
with a cereal box in her bed. But don't worry,
I got her back.

I carved I AM A in the bottom of her right
shoe with my pocketknife and PIG in her left. In
the morning when we walked across the field to
the chapel, she left her mark in the damp dirt.
I AM A   PIG. I AM A   PIG. I AM A   PIG.

What are you doing, anyway? It must be
boring without me. No offense or anything, but I'm
the one that comes up with all the good ideas.

Do you miss me? It's hard to know who you
like and who you don't because you're so nice to
everyone all the time. There ought to be a rule
against that. The Doormat Rule.

But maybe don't change too much, okay? If I
had a favorite person (which of course I don't!),
it would be you.

                              Yours truly,
                              Piper

"The Doormat Rule? How flattering." I hand the letter back to her.

We start up the hill again. Piper turns around and walks with us.

I invited her to come, but now it feels awkward. Am I really her favorite person? When the counterfeiting scheme came apart, Piper clung to my hand like a little kid. Sometimes it seems like all Piper wants is a friend; she just doesn't know how to keep one.

"I heard you were babysitting to pay your dad back," Jimmy says.

"Supposed to, but nobody exactly signed up. Now I'm expected to stay in the house all the time."

We've climbed up the hill far enough that we're looking down on the brown, hatlike roof of the dock guard tower. I'm pretty sure Trixle is in there today. I always feel uneasy when he's our guard. I mean, Darby Trixle with a Thompson automatic trained down on us ... that can't be good. But Warden Williams likes him no matter what he does. Everyone thinks it's because of his wife, Bea Trixle. Bea finds grocery deals like nobody's business. And that makes Warden Williams's expense report look good to the BOP—the Bureau of Prisons, the people the warden reports to.

When we get to Piper's, nobody wants to go inside. We set the game up on the warden's stoop, but it's pretty windy. We look for bricks and stones to anchor the card stacks and start playing. Piper is Machine Gun Kelly. She has to go back seven spaces, on account of they couldn't get her cellhouse door open, when the real Fastball appears, a dusting rag in his hand. His sharp eyes take us in.

"Your mother has been looking for you," he whispers to Piper.

"Well, here I am," Piper mumbles, her eyes on her game piece, the tiny machine gun.

"I see that," Fastball tells her. "So this is it?" He kneels down to inspect our game.

We can't hardly wait to show him everything, including the snitch cards, which have impossible choices like Should you turn in your best friend for keeping contraband in his cell, or go to a seg cell (what cons call "the hole") yourself?

"Hey, do any of the cells have a view of San Francisco?" I ask.

"A few do. Heck of a price to pay for a good view. You stick with baseball, you hear me?"

"Don't worry," I say.

"Wait a minute." Fastball frowns. "How come you don't have a legal way to get off the island?"

"A legal way?" Jimmy squints at him.

"We've never seen a prisoner get released from here. They always go to other prisons . . . ," I offer.

The smile drops off Fastball's face. His ears turn red. "Well, that's wrong," he says.

"We didn't make up the rules," I say.

"Yes, you did," he points out.

"Yeah, okay, we made up the rules for the game, but not the real ones," I say.

Fastball gets up from the stoop, wipes his hands on his pants, and goes inside.

We all look at each other.

"I didn't think he'd be so sensitive," I say.

Piper neatens the snitch-card stack. "He's up for parole."

"Really?"

"Uh-huh. Could get released or could make a wrong move and spend the rest of his life locked up." She motions her head to the cell house.

"What kind of wrong move?"

Piper spins the spinner. "Anything, really."

"Anything?"

She shrugs. "He could oversleep. They could find food in his cell. Some guard could decide they don't like him and write him up for something he didn't do. Happens all the time."

"That's not fair," I say.

"Nobody said prison was fair. None of the guys in there have rights."

I sit back. "But that's *wrong*. You should talk to your father about that."

She spins the spinner faster. "He's not going to listen to me."

"Fastball is a good guy, you know, for a bank robber. He should have a chance."

"It's just the way it works, Moose."

I stare up at the sky above the cell house. It's the only free part of this entire island. I wonder how often the cons even see it.

What would it be like to go years without seeing a star?

3. MY BARBER IS A DEAD GUY

■ ■

Wednesday, May 27, 1936

Early the next morning, Bea Trixle knocks on the door. "Yoo-hoo, Moose! Phone."

I stumble out with no shoes and my shirt buttoned wrong. I whip by Bea, run across the balcony, and leap down the stairs two at a time.

"For goodness' sake, Moose," Bea calls after me, "tell your friends not to call so early."

The phone is dangling on the cord outside the apartment where Mrs. Caconi used to live. It's Scout, my best school buddy. He starts talking before I get the receiver to my ear. "I got us a chance. Bring your Alcatraz stuff to school today."

"What . . . why?"

"I ran into Beck. He's the captain. He doesn't believe you live there, but he's interested in Alcatraz."

I don't see how Alcatraz is going to get us on the high school baseball team. But if anyone can wangle a way on, it's Scout. He can charm a tree stump. He can befriend a highway divider. He can convince a pen to become a pencil for the day.

"So?" I kick at a cigarette butt somebody left down here. "Nobody ever believes I live on Alcatraz."

"Freshmen don't get on the team. They just don't. We got to work every angle."

I pull the receiver away and give my ear a good scratch. "First we have to play better than they do. Doesn't this Beck guy want to see us play?"

"If we were sophomores, maybe . . . but freshmen? Not a chance. Look, I know you don't like trotting out your prison stuff, but could you please, this once?"

What do I say to that? "Sure, yeah, okay."

When I get back to my apartment, my mother and Natalie are already gone. Under the saltshaker I find a note.

Moose, Four more days to go! Love, Mom

I can't help smiling at this. I didn't realize she knew I was counting the last days of school. I like when my mom acts like my mom. Sometimes it seems like all she thinks about is Natalie.

In my room, I paw through my bureau. Crammed in the corner of my top drawer is a letter my gram sent. The envelope is addressed *Moose Flanagan, Alcatraz Island, California.* I stuff that in my pocket.

On top of my parents' dresser I see a form. *Inmate: #85. Date: May 25, 1936. Reason: Have important information you will want to know.* All the inmates have numbers, and Alcatraz #85 is Al Capone. My father says Capone is always requesting meetings with the warden. He wants special treatment like he got in the prison in Atlanta. Naturally, the warden turns him down.

I pocket the request. I'll have it back before my father gets home. He won't even know I borrowed it.

In the desk drawer I find a photo of me and my dad on the island, but Dad isn't in uniform, so we look like tourists. Still, that gives me an idea. I grab his extra uniform jacket off the hanger, fold it up, and stick it in my baseball bag. Then I get the rest of my school stuff and head for the dock.

As soon as my feet hit the wooden planks, the dock officer, a man they call the Nose, comes over. The Nose got his name because once he smelled convicts' moonshine hidden in a fire extinguisher. He's the same size I am—almost six feet—with the same brownish-blondish hair and brown eyes. Everybody says I look like him.

"Warden said you need to go get Piper," he tells me.

"I have to go to school."

"She can't go with you?"

"She doesn't go to my school anymore."

"Okay." He nods. "I'll let him know."

Sheesh. Am I going to have to spend every waking minute with her?

I stew about this all the way to school and throughout my morning classes. When lunch rolls around, I pull out my Alcatraz stash, and Scout and I huddle to sort out the right order in which to show everything. My afternoon classes go as slow as the morning ones. The closer we get to freedom, the harder it is to concentrate.

After the last bell, Scout and I cut out of there, running by a truck with a houseful of stuff tied on the back. A big Ford stops at the stop sign, motor rumbling. A man peddling cigarette butts taps on the window. Yesterday I saw a kid drop ice cream, and a man with newspaper shoes licked it up from the sidewalk. Things are tough out there. There are no jobs. Dad's got his money on President Roosevelt pulling us out of this depression, but so far things haven't changed that much.

When Scout has to wait to cross the street, I catch up. He leans over, panting. "I forgot to ask . . . is Piper back?"

Scout knows Piper on account of she used to go to school with us.

"Uh-huh."

"She look the same?"

"Pretty much."

His face is shiny with sweat. He runs his fingers through his crazy hair. "You still like her, or you're stuck on Annie?"

"Piper is trouble. Annie and I broke up."

"Annie dumped you?"

A man on a bicycle weaves through traffic. "No."

"Oh, I understand, you fell down in the kissing department and—" He makes a motion like he's slitting his throat with his finger.

"We decided *both of us*."

"A double dump? C'mon, Moose, that's as rare as a woman with three lips."

"Where exactly would the third lip go?"

"Two on the top. One on the bottom. Come on, did Annie dump you, or did you dump her?"

I trot along beside him. "She's my friend. It got complicated."

"Funny how you broke up with Annie just before Piper came back."

"That has nothing to do with—" I shout, but he's taken off again.

I chase him the rest of the way to the park. When we get close, his voice drops to a whisper. "There they are." He motions to a group of guys warming up.

What I notice first is how the high school boys fill out their shirts like sand poured in a bag. I'm big, too, but not solid like that.

Scout points to a guy with slicked-back blond hair and a look on his face like somebody insulted his sister. His joints move like butter as he winds up to throw the ball across the field. "That's Beck.

"The one over there with the pinhead, that's Dewey. He does everything Beck tells him to. On the first bag, the Italian lover boy, he's Passerini."

Normally, I can't tell if a guy is handsome or not. I mean, who knows? They're guys. But in Passerini's case, there's little doubt. With his tan skin, dark black hair, and dark eyes, every part of Passerini looks good with every other part.

"Let me do the talking." Scout shoots forward. "Hey, Beck!"

Beck glances at us. He cracks his elbow and then winds up for another throw. "Scout, my man."

Scout stands up straighter. "This is Moose. Remember, I told you about him. He plays first base."

The ball spins toward Beck. He folds it into his glove and sends it back. "Like I said . . . team's full up."

"How 'bout we warm up with you? Just so you know what you're missing," Scout wheedles.

Beck shakes his head. "Sorry, little man."

Scout's nostrils flare. He walks closer to Beck. "You should see Moose play. Criminals taught him everything he knows."

Beck winds up and lets the ball fly. Then he turns and gives me a once-over.

"You live on Alcatraz?"

"Yep," Scout answers for me. "He and Al Capone are buddies."

The sun goes behind a cloud. Beck spits on the ground. "I didn't ask you, Scout. I asked him."

"I live on Alcatraz," I say.

Beck catches the ball. Holds it in his glove. "Your father a prisoner?"

"No, my father's the assistant warden."

"Why you live with prisoners, then?"

"We don't live *with* them. We're on the same island is all. I've never even been in the cell house. Wouldn't want to go in, either. It gives me the creeps just walking by."

"Can't be that bad." Beck throws the ball. He moves like a well-oiled machine.

"The cruelest, most dangerous men in the entire country are all under one roof. . . . It's not exactly a picnic."

"Why you live so near to them, then?"

"If there's a problem in the cell house, the warden needs his guards close by."

"What kind of a problem?" The ball pops back into Beck's glove.

"An escape, a murder, an assassination, a conspiracy, something like that," Scout chimes in.

"That right?" Beck asks me.

I nod. "My father says every man in prison thinks of escaping. Some of them think of it some of the time. Some of them think of it all the time."

"Nice, huh?" Scout grins, sidling closer to Beck.

Beck turns and faces us. "You got proof you live there? Or you shooting your mouth off?"

I dig in my baseball bag.

Beck walks closer.

The breeze cools the sweat on the back of my neck.

"Go slow. Milk it," Scout says under his breath.

I take out the letter from my grandma.

Beck hands the envelope to Dewey, who passes it down the line to the other guys who have come in from the field. It doesn't make much of an impression.

Next thing I bring out is the form. They don't give this a second look, either: #85 doesn't mean anything to them.

"Alcatraz number 85 is Al Capone," I explain.

"How do we know his number is 85? You got proof?"

"No . . . but it is," I say.

Beck shrugs and hands the form down the line.

I pull out my father's uniform jacket and hand it to Beck.

He runs his hands over it, then slips his arms into the sleeves. He pats the collar down and struts around the base bag, cocking his head to the left and the right.

Dewey nods. "Looks good."

Beck arches his back and sticks his hands deep in the pockets. "Hey." He pulls a folded scrap of paper out of the left pocket.

Everyone crowds around Beck as he unfolds the paper.

"Whose side are you on?" he reads.

Beck scrutinizes me. "You put that in there?"

"Nope."

His eyelids lower. "You must have."

"I didn't."

"Well, what's it doing in there?"

"I don't know. The convicts do our laundry. Al Capone works the mangle. He's the guy who wrote it." This is true. I know Capone's handwriting, but how do I make them believe it?

Beck rolls his eyes. "Yeah, and Dillinger was my uncle."

Passerini grins, tossing the ball from one hand to the other. "Machine Gun Kelly is my postman."

"Bonnie and Clyde are my barbers," Scout says.

"Bonnie and Clyde are dead. So is Dillinger," I inform them.

"No wonder their fingers are so cold." Scout's hands creep through his hair. "You ever have a dead guy cut your hair? It feels strange."

Everybody laughs.

I search the circle of faces. "I've never played ball with the convicts. I'm not allowed in the rec yard where they play. Criminals haven't taught me anything . . . but that right there is a note from Al Capone."

Beck squints at me. He kicks the base bag. "It doesn't have his number on it."

"He doesn't want people to know it's him."

Beck rolls his eyes. "Convenient."

Dewey rolls his eyes just like Beck.

"No, it's true. I swear."

Beck fingers my dad's jacket. "What's it mean, anyway? What sides is he talking about?"

"I don't know," I admit.

"Why would Capone send a note to you if you don't know what it means?" Beck's beady eyes fix on me.

"He sent it to my dad," I say as a pigeon scuttles by my foot.

Beck licks his lip. "Tell you what. . . . Get a photo of you and Scarface Capone, and you and Scout can play."

"What? I can't get a picture of Al Capone and me. That's crazy."

Scout reaches up to put his hand over my mouth. "Sure he can," he tells Beck.

"Scout?" I pull his fingers off. "What am I supposed to do, get a portrait photographer in his cell?"

Beck takes the jacket off and hands it back to me. "That's your problem."

Dewey takes a step closer. "You don't really know Capone, do you?"

"Yes, I do . . . but he's in prison. You know, locked up. It's not like I see him every day."

Beck shrugs. He motions with his head, and Dewey, Passerini, and the other guys trot back out to the field.

The shadows are long and cool, the sun not too hot. My glove is in my bag, waiting for my hand.

Scout grins at me. "That was easy."

"Are you nuts?"

Scout slips on his glove. "If Al's your friend, he'll help you."

"It's prison, not a women's club. I can't get my picture taken with Al Capone."

"I know, okay." Scout tosses the ball to me before I even get my glove on. "But you'll think of something, Moose. You always do."

4. THE BIGGEST NOSY PARKER

. . . .

Wednesday, May 27, 1936

I'm still fuming about Scout when I climb the stairs to our apartment. I know he wants to be on the team as badly as I do, but a photo with Al Capone? Scout's been to Alcatraz. He knows that's not possible.

And what was that note from Capone supposed to mean, anyway? *Whose side are you on?* What is he trying to tell my father?

When I get to my door, Piper is sitting outside, waiting for me. She's the last person I want to see. Whatever charm she has isn't working on me right now.

"You're supposed to be watching me."

"I was at school and then baseball practice."

"When are you out for the summer?"

"Monday's the last day."

"That's a weird last day," she says.

I shrug, letting myself into my apartment, which is eerily quiet, nothing but floating dust motes. Nat must not be home yet. I can't help but be a little relieved. I don't want to have to deal with Piper *and* Nat right now.

Piper follows me inside.

"Mom?" I call. Her music bag sits on the kitchen counter. Her bedroom door is closed.

I knock. She doesn't answer.

"Mom?" I try again.

I've just turned away when I hear her voice, thin as chicken broth. "Come in."

I slip inside and close the door behind me so Piper won't follow. My mom is lying in bed with her arm over her face.

"You okay?" I ask.

She doesn't answer.

"Mom?"

"I've got a headache. Just give me a minute."

Uh-oh ... did something happen? My mom gets headaches when things aren't going well with Natalie. Is it because today is Natalie's birthday?

"When's Natalie coming home?"

"Six-thirty," my mom murmurs, turning toward the wall. "Carrie Kelly's bringing her."

Carrie Kelly is a lady who helps Natalie learn how to do stuff. She works part-time for the Esther P. Marinoff and part-time for us. In the past few months, Carrie Kelly has been really happy with Natalie's progress.

Last week Nat stood at the door of the Esther P. Marinoff and shook every person's hand. The week before, a kid was having a tantrum, and Natalie got down on the floor with her and showed her how she lies on her hands when she gets upset. Nat's own tantrums haven't gone away, but they are shorter, and she gets over them more quickly.

"Mom? Did you buy a cake, or are you going to bake one?"

My sister loves lemon cake. We can't have her birthday without one.

My mom doesn't answer.

I go back into the kitchen.

"What's the matter?" Piper asks.

"Nothing," I mumble.

Piper's eyebrows do a little dance.

She always knows what's up with me. It's like my face is a picture window she can see right through.

I don't want to tell her any more than I have to. She doesn't need to know I'm worried there won't be a birthday cake for Natalie.

I consider asking Mrs. Mattaman to bake one. The Mattamans have the same kitchen setup we do. The same icebox and stove. The same sink and broom closet. But Mrs. Mattaman's kitchen is stuffed to bursting with flour and spices, cans of olive oil, sugar and rolling pins, measuring cups and cookie cutters. The Mattaman kitchen smells like butter and garlic or like chocolate cake or pumpkin bread. Our kitchen smells like nothing right now.

If I ask Mrs. Mattaman, she'll know something is wrong at my house. If I had money, I'd take the ferry to San Francisco and buy a bakery cake.

Maybe I should call Dad. I imagine him in the middle of restraining a lunatic killer who has blown up the toilet in his cell when he gets a message from his son about birthday cake.

On the kitchen counter are canisters of flour and sugar; in the icebox, butter and eggs. I've never made a cake, but it can't be that hard.

What else do I need? Lemons? Baking powder? Or is it baking soda?

Piper leans on her elbows, watching me.

"Don't you have somewhere else to go?" I ask.

"You're supposed to be my bodyguard."

"I'm busy."

"Doesn't look like it."

I turn away from her. "Yeah, well, I am. I'm baking a cake."

She bursts out in great peals of laughter.

"Shut up. I am."

"Do you have a recipe?"

I can feel my cheeks get hot. Why didn't I think of that? I knock on Mom's door. "Mom, where are your recipes?"

She doesn't answer.

I head outside, Piper on my heels. "Let's go down to the canteen," I tell her.

Bea Trixle is standing in her usual spot behind the cash register. From here, she runs the canteen, her home beauty salon, and the lives of everybody who lives on Alcatraz. Bea is the biggest nosy parker. She collects gossip the way a gutter collects rain.

Her hair is shoulder length and rusty red today, the color of baked beans. Baked beans are on special this month. I think that's why.

"Why, Piper ... hello, honey." Bea gives her a hug and whispers loud enough for me to hear. "Your daddy talk to you yet?"

Piper's cheeks get red. She ducks behind the canned-goods display.

Bea turns to me. "Is your sister home yet, Moose? Your mother's been after me to cut her hair for her birthday. Wants it just like this." Bea reaches in her apron for a page clipped from a magazine. The photo is of a kindergarten-age girl. She has hair curled into ringlets and pulled back with an enormous pink ribbon.

"She'll be home later," I mutter, wondering why my mom would suggest this. Natalie can't tolerate having her hair messed with. Besides, Bea Trixle isn't exactly Natalie's greatest fan. Once, when there was a fire in our apartment, Bea blamed Natalie. She was really mean about it, too—she acted like Natalie was guilty without any evidence. That's always the way it is with Natalie. Anything bad happens, people blame her.

My father says it's because people don't grasp the way she thinks. He says people villainize what they don't understand. To me, it just seems cruel.

"You send her in after closing, and I'll get her fixed up."

I remember once my dad said when it comes to women and their hair, there's no rhyme or reason, and the sooner a man realizes this, the better off he'll be.

I go up and down the cramped aisles, looking for baking soda and baking powder. I'll put in both. There's no such thing as a cake that rises too much, right?

Then I get lemons.

Piper gets two pops and sets them on the counter.

Bea surveys my items. "Baking soda and baking powder?" She frowns at me.

I shrug like I have no idea why my mom would want this.

Bea records all my costs on a worn yellow card that says

FLANAGAN at the top. She writes Piper's two sodas on the WILLIAMS card. On payday, the dads come in to pay off their tabs. Bea Trixle has a big, fat grin on her face that day.

"Everything okay?" Bea squints at me.

"Yes, ma'am." I stuff a lemon in my pocket. No way I'm having a conversation with Bea Trixle about my mother.

Bea looks over at Piper for confirmation.

Piper smiles innocently, her attention on the bottle opener attached to the side of the counter. She pops the caps of both bottles.

When we get outside, the gulls are making a lot of noise. They always sound like they're calling their friends to a funeral. They love our island.

"Have you ever made a cake before?" Piper shouts the birds down.

"Not exactly."

"Is it for Natalie's birthday?"

"Maybe," I mumble as the bird cries subside and a ferryboat toots in the distance.

"We can get a recipe from Fastball. He'll keep his mouth shut," she says.

I grind my teeth. I can see this is a good idea. But why does she have to figure everything out? I run up and deposit the groceries, then meet her at the back of 64. We start up the steep switchback to her house. She hands me one of her pops.

"Hey, thanks," I say as the count bell rings.

We swig our sodas. I hate to admit it, but it's kind of nice walking together, drinking pop, and not saying too much. That's the trouble with Piper. Sometimes she's really nice. You just can't count on her to stay that way.

We're just past Doc Ollie's house when I spot Theresa hiding in the warden's garden. Piper sees her, too. It's not a great place to hide, as the most important gardening rule on Alcatraz is *No bush can grow tall enough to hide behind.*

"What are you doing?" I call out.

Theresa hops out of the garden. "Nothing," she mutters.

"Why are you spying on me?" Piper asks.

Theresa's hands are on her hips; the wind blows her crazy-curly hair. "You know why."

Piper faces Theresa. "I'm sorry about what I did, okay?"

Theresa stares Piper down.

Piper offers her pop to Theresa. Theresa takes the bottle, closes one eye, and peers inside. "You're not sorry."

"Yeah, I am," Piper says.

Theresa frowns at her.

"My father is still so mad, he can't look me in the eye. My mom acts like she wishes I would dig a hole and crawl in."

"Are you sorry because they're mad? Or are you sorry because you're sorry?" Theresa demands.

Pretty good question for an eight-year-old.

I watch Piper closely, wondering what she'll say.

"I hate boarding school. But at least there, people give me a chance. All anyone here remembers is the one thing I did wrong."

"Yeah, but are you sorry?" Theresa asks.

"I wish I hadn't done what I did, if that's what you mean. But"—her eyes harden—"I don't see why everyone got quite so upset about it."

Theresa and I exchange a look.

Piper watches this. "I'm not going to do it again, if that's what you're worried about."

Theresa nods.

Piper's face softens. "Moose has forgiven me, right, Moose?"

"Yeah," I say, and when the word comes out, I realize it's true. I have forgiven her.

Theresa takes a swig of pop, wipes her mouth with the back of her hand, and passes it back. "Okay."

"Thank you," Piper asks.

Theresa nods, and we start walking again. "So, what are you going to do about it?"

"About what?" Piper asks.

"About how everybody hates you," Theresa says.

"I dunno. But whatever it is, it's got to be good," she says.

When we get to Piper's house, she opens the door, and Mrs. Williams comes rushing down the stairs. "Where were you?" she demands.

"Waiting for Moose," Piper tells her.

"All afternoon?"

"I didn't know when he'd be home."

Mrs. Williams turns to me. "I hate putting you in the middle of this, Moose, but I don't know what else to do. Was she waiting for you when you got home?"

"Yes, ma'am," I say.

"Well . . ." Mrs. Williams sighs. "That's something."

Piper arches her eyebrow as if to say "I told you so." She leads the way to the kitchen.

Fastball is kneeling on a dishrag, scrubbing the floor with a sudsy brush.

"Hi." Piper smiles at Fastball. "We were wondering if you had a good recipe for lemon cake. Moose wants to"—Piper looks at me—"surprise his sister."

I nod to Piper, grateful for how she phrased this. "A surprise for my sister" sounds a lot better than "I'm baking a cake because my mother is too upset to do it herself."

"My mom has a recipe, Moose. You didn't have to come all the way up here," Theresa says. "Hey! What's that?"

"What's what?" Piper asks.

Theresa stares at the kitchen door. "That scratching."

Fastball hoists himself up, walks to the kitchen door, and cracks it open. In scoots a black kitten barely bigger than a baseball. The kitten has white paws and a white nose. He winds around Fastball's leg and scratches his claws on his shoe. Fastball leans down and scoops him up.

Theresa starts jumping around. "That was it! That was the sound I heard."

"What sound . . . ? Oh, when you thought the escaped convict was scratching at your door. That is one small convict," I say.

Theresa grins. "Can I pet him?"

"Sure." Fastball offers the kitten to Theresa to hold. "*Her* name is Bug."

"Wait—Bug was all the way down at 64 Building?" Piper asks.

"Probably smelled Mrs. Mattaman's cooking. Smart cat," I say.

Everybody laughs.

"Where'd she come from?" I ask, stroking Bug's soft, fluffy fur.

"We don't know, exactly," Fastball says.

Theresa snuggles her against her chest.

Piper reaches out and rubs Bug's tiny velvety nose. "Somebody might have dumped her on the island. Or remember those stray cats that used to be down at the west beach? Maybe one of them had kittens."

Theresa hands Bug back to Fastball, who slides her into his shirt pocket. Bug stretches her paws upward and hangs around his neck with a squeaking meow. Fastball walks with her to the icebox, pours a saucer of milk, and then sets her down with it.

Bug sticks her nose all the way in, then pulls it out and laps the milk off her face. We all laugh.

Fastball takes a wooden box from the pantry and thumbs through the recipe cards. When he finds what he's looking for, he hands me the card. "Won't find a better lemon cake than that one, with all due respect to Mrs. Mattaman."

"Thanks." I slip the card in my pocket and glance at the clock. How long does it take to bake a cake?

Theresa watches Bug stir the milk with her paw.

I look over at Fastball. "Hey, did you really play in the minor leagues?"

"Yup." His eyes don't meet mine.

I'm guessing Fastball is in his late forties, though it's hard to tell how old adults are. He looks older than my dad but not as old as my grandpa.

How can he stand being in prison year after year, watching his body get old and his dream dry up and blow away? How can he forgive himself?

"What was it like . . . in the minors?"

Fastball's eyes flicker with something I haven't seen in them before. "Competitive. I wanted to move up so badly, I could taste it. But I'll tell you what, you play with men who have that kind of talent, your game gets better. It has to."

I think about Beck, Dewey, and Passerini.

"Some days it went so well, I thought I was untouchable." His face darkens. His eyes turn smoky. "That was a long time ago."

"But you still play, right?"

His eye twitches. "In the rec yard," he mutters.

Must feel pretty lousy to play prison ball when you've been in the minors. Got to be even worse than going back to your junior high team when you're in high school.

I wonder what it would be like to play against Fastball. How much better is he than me?

Fastball gives me a long, hungry look. "I'd be grateful if you put in a good word with your father."

"My father? It's her father." I point my thumb toward Piper.

Fastball scoops Bug up and slips her back in his pocket. He doesn't look at Piper.

Piper bites her lip. Her nostrils flare.

"He doesn't think my dad will listen to me," Piper says. "But that will change. You wait."

5. WHOSE SIDE ARE YOU ON?

■ ■

Wednesday, May 27, 1936

When I get home, I'm relieved to see my father sitting in his chair with a bowl of peanuts and a glass of tomato juice.

"Where's Mom?" I ask.

"Getting herself together."

"How come she didn't bake a cake?"

My dad scoops peanuts into his palm. "She must have bought one."

"Uh-uh."

My father finishes chewing and wipes his mouth. "You sure?"

"Yes, but don't worry. I got a recipe and the stuff we need to bake one." I set the recipe on the table.

His smile looks tired. "I'll check into it. I didn't get a chance to ask you last night . . . what happened with the warden yesterday?"

"He wants me to babysit Piper."

"Ohhhh. What did you say?"

"I tried to say no, but . . ."

"The warden is a hard man to say no to. You want me to back you up?"

I shake my head. "I kind of feel bad for Piper. He's so mad at her."

Dad chews a toothpick. "When he found out she was mixed up in that racket, it just about killed him."

"I remember."

He nods. "Just be sure you don't bite off more than you can chew. I know you want to work on your game this summer. You play today?"

I shake my head. "The high school guys haven't exactly let Scout and me on the team yet."

"Ah, well"—he takes a gulp of tomato juice—"I guess things haven't changed much since I was in high school."

I consider telling him what they asked me to do, but I know what he'll say. A photo with Al Capone? Never going to happen.

When he goes to the kitchen, I put the form back on the dresser and his jacket in the closet. I'd like to ask him about the note, but I can't explain why I borrowed his jacket, and I can't say I was going through his pockets.

Dad stirs his tomato juice with a celery stalk and walks back into the living room, when the front door flies open and Natalie and Carrie Kelly bustle in.

Of course Natalie wouldn't knock, but it seems odd that Mrs. Kelly wouldn't. With steel-gray hair and a steel-gray heart, she is one tough lady. She loves Natalie, though. That's for sure.

My father jumps out of his seat. "Sweet pea. Happy birthday, love!"

"Happy birthday, happy birthday," Natalie drones, looking down at her feet as she counts her steps from the door.

"Natalie, look at your father when you speak," Mrs. Kelly tells her.

Natalie's eyes shoot in his direction, then swing back across the room like a searchlight. Eventually they settle on him, and in that split second, she smiles, a quick half smile like a rainbow you see for a second.

Dad's face lights up.

"Good," Mrs. Kelly says under her breath.

My mother appears, wearing her go-to-the-city dress, her hair combed and fresh lipstick on. "Will you stay for supper?" she asks.

Mrs. Kelly shakes her head. "I wish I could, but I have to go home and pack. I'm going to see my brother. But I'm very pleased with how you're doing, Natalie," she says to Nat, and then turns to us. "Yesterday, I was talking to a neighbor in the lobby of my building. I thought Natalie was behind me, but when I turned around, she'd struck up a conversation with the doorman."

"Really?" my mom asks.

"Yes," Mrs. Kelly says as Bea knocks on the door, then comes right in. "Yoo-hoo. I'm Bea Trixle."

Mrs. Kelly takes Bea's hand and gives it a no-nonsense shake. "I've heard about you."

"Of course you have," Bea announces. "Moose, did you tell your mama I'd do Natalie's hair?"

"No, ma'am," I say.

Bea gives me a look like I broke her best teacup. She turns to my mom. "Oh, honey, you must be so happy to have your girl turning seventeen."

"I am, thank you, Bea." My mother's words are brittle.

"Oh my, look at the time. . . ." Carrie Kelly glances at her watch. "I have to skedaddle or I'll miss the boat. Have fun, Natalie. Happy birthday!" She squeezes past Bea.

"She's such a pretty girl, your Natalie," Bea tells my mom when Mrs. Kelly is gone. "She really is."

Mom's eyes glow.

"But she does need a haircut," Bea says.

I bite my lip, waiting for my mom to tell her to forget about it, but Mom turns to Natalie. "What do you think, Nat? Do you want a new hairstyle?"

"New hairstyle," Natalie mumbles, her eyes down.

Does Natalie mean she wants a new hairstyle, or is she just repeating Mom's words? You never know with her.

My mom flashes a smile at Bea. "Why, I guess she does."

"Super!" Bea belts out. "Got time in half an hour. Will that work?"

My father and mother exchange a look.

"That is kind of you, Bea, but I don't think we're quite ready—" my father starts.

Natalie heads for the light switch, flicking it on and off, on and off. "New hairstyle. New hairstyle."

We all stare at her in the flickering light.

Nat kneads her lip with her teeth, lifts her chin, and stares straight into my father's eyes. "I would like a hairstyle *today*."

"I'll be darned. . . ." Mom's voice is hoarse.

"Wow, that was good." My father beams. "Good job, sweet pea."

"I'll tell you what"—Bea grins—"your little lady knows what she wants. Well, good. Glad we got that squared away. See you in half an hour."

After Bea goes, my mother and my father exchange a look. "It was nice of her to offer," Dad says.

"What if she pitches a fit? Bea will tell everyone on the island about it. You know she will," I say.

Mom nods. "Yep. On top of that, it will make supper awfully late, and birthdays are challenging enough." She gets up and goes into the kitchen.

"This is what she wants, Helen." My father's voice is firm.

My mom sighs, then sticks her head out. "I guess it won't take too long. Twenty, thirty minutes. You can stand right there, Moose, and if anything happens, you can get her out of there."

"Me? *I* will? This is girl business, Mom."

"Your mother is exhausted, Moose," my father says.

"Moose take me," Nat mutters. "Moose, Moose, Moose."

I look to my dad for help. "What about the cake?" I whisper.

He taps the tips of his fingers together. "I'll take care of it. Look, let's roll with the punches here, Moose. Natalie's the boss today. It's her birthday, and she wants you to go."

"What cake?" My mother sticks her head back in the living room.

"We have to have a birthday cake, Mom," I say.

"Who says?" Mom mutters.

"Helen?" my father warns. Then he turns to me: "You go on, Moose. I'll handle this."

6. TRIXLE TRICKS

▪ ▪

Wednesday, May 27, 1936

I'm following Natalie up the stairs to the Trixles' apartment when I hear her mumble: "Sad. Mommy sad."

I stop in the landing. "What did you say?"

She spins around in a circle. "Sad Mommy."

Nat never says things like that. She has trouble figuring out what other people feel.

"Yes," I say. "Mom is sad."

She keeps spinning, her hands flying out. "Why?"

Do I tell her the truth, that her birthday depresses our mom? Or make something up?

"She worries about us getting older," I finally say.

Nat slows down. "Mommy can't count."

"What? Oh." I smile. Funny it's never occurred to me how it must have driven Natalie nuts to have Mom miscount her age every year.

"Yeah," I say. "You got to count for her. You're the family counter."

Does she smile? It was so quick I don't know if I saw it or made it up. She heads up the last set of stairs to the third floor.

The door to the Trixles' apartment is propped open. The kitchen stinks of peroxide and hair chemicals. Natalie is sensitive to smells, loud noises, and bright lights. How's she going to stand this? Even I can't handle it. But Nat walks right in.

I hold my breath and follow her.

"Hairstyle," Nat mumbles.

Bea is wearing a pink apron with rows of hair clips hanging from the pockets. A kitchen chair is stuck in the middle of the floor. Piper, her hair tied in a red kerchief, stands by the sink, scrubbing a pot. When I see her, my heart jumps a little. Why is she in Bea Trixle's kitchen?

Bea motions that Natalie should sit down and then flings a blue smock around her shoulders. Natalie shudders. "New hairstyle," she mutters. "Stay quiet."

Wow . . . Nat's trying to calm herself? I've never seen her do that before.

"All righty then." Bea wets a comb under the faucet and sinks the teeth into Nat's hair.

I cross my fingers, hoping this goes well. Nat likes her hair combed as much as I like an all-day algebra test. She's pitched some whopper fits around getting her hair fixed, and Bea isn't gentle with the snarls. I can't watch. I turn away. "What are you doing here?" I ask Piper.

Piper wipes her hands on a dish towel and straightens her kerchief. "Working for Bea."

"I am the only person on this whole island willing to give her a chance. *The only one!*" Bea crows, waving her comb at Piper.

"Yes, ma'am," Piper says politely, but behind Bea's back, she flutters her eyelids like she's having a fit and mouths the words "the only one."

I grin.

"Now, Natalie, how old are you today, sweetheart?" Bea asks.

"Seventeen," Nat mumbles.

"Lordy, lordy," Bea harrumphs. She takes the magazine picture out of her pocket and flutters it in my face. "This is not the hairstyle of a seventeen-year-old girl."

For once, I agree with Bea.

"Seventeen-year-old girl," Nat echoes.

"Exactly. You and I, Natalie, we're on the same page. Your mother is just ... well, she's your mother. We'll get you all fixed up here. Oh yes, we will."

"All fixed up," Nat says under her breath.

Bea's lips are bright as tropical flowers. "It's lucky you came to old Bea. That's all I can say."

Bea sets to work, snipping and combing until scraps of blond-brown hair are scattered on the floor around Nat's chair.

Piper runs water into the pot, sloshes it around, and then starts scrubbing. Nat's nose twitches. She begins to squirm.

"Piper!" Bea mumbles through the comb in her mouth. "Can you help us out here?"

She's asking Piper to help? That's a mistake.

But Piper picks up a piece of paper and draws out a grid of dots, then patiently explains the rules of the game to Natalie.

Soon the paper is a grid of dots and squares with *P* or *N* written in them. Then Bea waves her scissors at me. "Moose, can you take over? Piper is due at Jimmy's. He's going to show her the ropes."

"You're working with Jimmy?" I ask.

"For now," Bea answers for Piper.

Piper and I exchange a look. Does *for now* mean Piper's not going to be working for Bea anymore, or Jimmy isn't?

Bea loves to fire people. She's sacked Jimmy twice. But she always hires him back. He's the only one who can do the books. Jimmy has to put up with whatever she dishes out. It's impossible to get a job as a kid when there are so many grown men out of work. My father is lucky. All the guards on Alcatraz feel that way. Most everyone here is overqualified. We've got two guards with graduate degrees, one who was a lawyer, and a bunch of ex-bankers.

"Don't you look sweet," Bea says, combing out Nat's new hairdo. She shakes her scissors at Piper. "Go on, now. We don't have all night. Jimmy's got to teach you, and then I told your mama you'd be home for dinner. You follow my lead, I'll get you back in your daddy's good graces. Oh, he loves me, yes, he does. Nobody can get him wholesale groceries as cheaply as I can."

"You'll tell him I'm doing a good job?" Piper asks.

"Oh now, I've got something up my sleeve. Don't you worry your pretty little head about that."

After Piper leaves, Bea natters on. "He loves that girl like there's no tomorrow. All she's got to do is straighten up and fly right, and he'll forgive her. You know he will."

"Yes, ma'am," I say.

"And you are pretty as a picture." Bea hands Natalie a mirror.

Nat's hair is cut just below her ears and has a wavy curl on one side, with a ribbon clipped on the other.

"There you go, missy. You're back in business." Bea unhooks Nat's smock and hangs it on the back of a chair. "Such a pretty girl."

"Thank you"—Nat's words are halting and stiff—"Bea Trixle."

"Now, you wait just a minute, I have a little birthday something for you." Bea trots into the living room and comes back with a gold box tied with a gold bow.

A gift for Natalie? When did Bea Trixle start being nice?

Bea hands the box to Natalie. Natalie slips it under her arm and heads for the door.

"What's she doing?" Bea whispers to me.

"She doesn't like to open her presents."

"Why not?"

"I dunno."

"Oh, for goodness' sake . . . you Flanagans." Bea wags her finger at me. "You don't tell this poor girl the first thing about how to behave. If she were my daughter, she'd know. You bet she would."

"Where is Janet, anyway?" Janet is Bea and Darby's only child.

"She's at the beach with my sister. Alcatraz is no place for a child to spend her summer. Betty Bomini and I agree on that. Course, your mother has her own ideas." Bea lifts up the hand mirror and takes a gander at herself, picking at her hair with her fingers.

"Go on, Moose, explain to your sister when she's given a gift, she should open it."

It's not like we haven't tried *that* before. "Natalie . . ." I wave my hand to get her attention.

Natalie's mouth pulls at her face. Then she takes the box out from under her arm, slips the bow off, and unwraps the paper.

My mouth hangs open. "Wow! Good job, Nat," I say, though honestly, I'm a little ticked off. We've only been trying to get Natalie to do this her whole life, and Bea acts like she's the only one who ever thought of it.

Nat opens the lid. She pulls a green dress out of the box.

"You got a nice little figure, young lady, and it's about time you showed it off," Bea crows, grinning from one big, round earring to the other. "You're going to want to snag a husband one of these days. You betcha."

"A nice figure, young lady." Natalie runs her fingers tenderly over the crisp, newly ironed dress, then slips her hand inside the lining. She touches the dress as if she can see it with her fingers.

She squirms, her arm doubled behind her. I walk to the door, thinking she'll follow me, but her feet are parked, and then suddenly her own dress sweeps over her head.

"Nat, no! Please! Not here! Jeez!"

Who wants to see his sister in her underwear?

Bea's face is red as a fire ant. "For goodness' sake, young lady. Hasn't your mother taught you anything?"

"Like the dress," Nat mutters, sticking her head through the neckline and wiggling her arms through the armholes. She pulls the sleek green dress over her waist and threads the belt through the loops.

"Where is your modesty?" Bea clucks. "I can't say I blame

you. Those silly little-girl dresses your mother has you wear. I'd want to tear them off, too. Come on over here. Let me get you fastened."

Bea buttons the back of the dress, presses the collar down, and tugs at the slip lining. Then she steps back, surveying Nat. "What you need is shoes."

Shoes?

Bea *click-clack*s into her room and comes back with two pairs of high-heeled shoes. She sets them on the floor. "There now."

Natalie pulls off her scuffed brown shoes and slips her feet in a green pair of high heels.

"What do you think, Moose?" Bea asks.

"Yeah, uh-huh. Look, we have to go, Bea, but thanks."

Bea's hands fly to her hips. "Slow down, mister. After I've gone to all this trouble, the least you can do is take a gander."

Bea drives me crazy. What does she think I've been doing? I make myself stop, turn, and look.

I swallow hard. Holy smokes. This is not Natalie.

"I could not have gotten a better fit if I'd had the tailor right here with us. I got an eye, oh yes, I do. You keep those shoes. They are perfect with it. But wait!" Bea runs out and comes back with lipstick. She draws color on Nat's lips, making them as pink as her own.

Bea grins like a pelican in a tuna run. She steps back. "There!" she says.

I open the door. Nat's watching her feet as she shuffles forward inch by inch.

"There you go. You're getting the hang of it. If I could only get your mother to buy you a proper brassiere." Bea sighs.

My skin feels hot, and my hives start itching. Only Bea would discuss my sister's underclothes with me.

"Thanks, Bea," I mumble, picking up Nat's old brown shoes and following her out the door.

"You better wear these," I tell her when we're outside. "Otherwise, it's going to take an hour just to get down the stairs."

Nat bites her lip and takes one tiny, sliding step after another.

7. THE RULE OF SILENCE

. . . .

Wednesday, May 27, 1936

I can smell the cake before I even open the door. Mom is in the living room, thumbing through the Sears catalog. When she looks up, she smiles at me. But then she sees Natalie. The catalog slips out of her hand and thuds onto the rug. "Oh!" Mom chokes.

"Bea gave her a different hairstyle and a new birthday dress. Nat's really excited about it." I'm talking fast. I can't look my mom in the eye.

Natalie teeters through the living room. "Such a pretty girl," she mutters, heading for the mirror in my parents' room.

My dad hurries out of the kitchen. "What's the matter?"

My mom shakes her head.

Dad goes into their room. The bedroom light streams out. His shape is dark against it. "Look at you, sweet pea!"

Dad offers his arm to Natalie, and she takes it! Arm in arm, they walk back into the living room.

For a girl who hates to be touched, this is amazing.

"I am seventeen today," Nat says.

"Yes, you are. What a nice birthday meal we're going to have."

Mom is pale. Her eyes are glazed.

"Meat loaf and lemon cake," Nat says.

"That's right, sweet pea." My father looks at my mother. "Helen." He motions toward their bedroom.

She follows him in. "For crying out loud, Cam . . ." My father shuts the door.

I can't make out what he's saying in response, but his voice is low and soothing.

Natalie slides into the kitchen and peeks into the oven.

A little later, Mom comes out and serves the meat loaf, biscuits, and broccoli my father brought from the cell house. She slips into her place at the table. We say grace and start eating.

My father keeps up a running conversation about Natalie. "Remember that time when you were in, what was it, Nat, fourth grade? I bet your teacher you could add the ages of every U.S. president on Inauguration Day, divide by the number of presidents, and get the average age of a U.S. president all in your head, and of course you did. Boy, was she surprised." He grins.

"Fifty-four and one-fourth," Nat says.

"That's a different answer than you gave her."

"We've had another president since then—Roosevelt," I point out.

"So we have. Do we have the most brilliant children in the world, Helen?"

My mom perks up. She refills the biscuit platter. When she comes back from the kitchen, there's a knock on the door. "Yoo-hoo, Flanagans!" Bea Trixle's nose presses against the window.

My father gets up and opens the door. "Hello, Bea."

"Cam, sorry to interrupt your supper. But it just occurred

to me what Natalie needs to complete her outfit." She dangles a green purse in his face.

"That's kind of you." My father's voice is warm. He doesn't fake being nice; he finds something he genuinely likes about everyone. "I can see you went all out for my girl on her big day."

Bea beams, inching across the threshold.

My father steps forward, blocking her.

Bea hands the purse to my father. "Oh, and by the way, Cam, you got any problems up top, you know Darby and me stand behind you. Oh yes, we do."

She waits, her mouth half open, her eyebrows arched.

"Thank you, Bea. I'll keep that in mind." He closes the door, sets the purse on the living room chair, and comes back to the table.

"What was that all about?" my mom asks.

"Oh, just Bea doing a little snooping."

"About what?"

My father sighs. "I expect she's angling to get Darby promoted. She's been giving me an earful about that. And she's heard we may have a strike. Can't say she's wrong." He picks up the butter knife and carves a slice of butter, which he spreads on his biscuit.

Natalie darts to the living room. She picks up the purse and carries it back to the table and holds it on her lap.

"Who's striking?" I ask.

Dad swallows a bite of biscuit. "Prisoners. Could be tomorrow. We'll know in the morning."

"Why are they striking?"

"They're objecting to the rule of silence."

The convicts aren't supposed to talk to each other. Not in their cells, not in the cafeteria, not at work. They aren't even supposed to on the rec yard, but not many guards enforce that.

I look at him. "You don't like that rule."

"I can't say I do. Seems cruel to me. Now." He pushes back from the table. "Miss Sweet Pea, will you forgive us for talking shop on your big day?"

"Big day." Nat carries her dish to the kitchen with one hand, Bea's purse hanging over the other.

She sets her dish down and heads for the cake, which doesn't have frosting. No time for that, I guess. I'm about to tell Natalie that Mom's not going to like it if she eats her cake in the kitchen. But then I see she isn't eating, she's sticking candles in it.

One, two, three, four, five, six, seven, eight, nine, ten, eleven, twelve, thirteen, fourteen, fifteen, sixteen, seventeen.

This is the first time Nat has had the correct number of candles on her cake. Every other year my mother has put on ten.

That's when I figure out why my mother didn't want to have a cake.

When we settle in the living room, I line up Nat's gifts on the coffee table. None are wrapped, though I wish now they were.

Nat is changing. We need to catch up.

I got her a purple pillow to match her favorite purple blanket. Dad and Mom bought her an abacus and a big, thick book: *All About the Moon*. It has a substantial index, of course—Nat's favorite part. And hanging on a hanger is a pink dress from my mom. It looks like a dress for an eight-year-old.

"Thank you," Nat says. But she doesn't touch any of our gifts. She carries Bea's green handbag to her button box and opens the clasp, and one by one she places her buttons inside.

When it's time for cake and my mom sees the candles, she takes a deep, raggedy breath. Her hands tremble as she lights all seventeen.

Nat blows out the candles, and my mother yanks them from the cake and cuts us each a piece. My mom is the only one who doesn't have cake.

While we're eating, Mom approaches Natalie. "Honey, that is such a nice dress that Bea gave you." She's trying to smile, but it looks more like a twitch. "But you should know it is only for special, special days. You don't want to ruin it."

Natalie skitters her fork back and forth along her empty plate.

At bedtime, she climbs in bed with Bea's dress on. She pulls up the covers and goes to sleep.

8. MILK AND COOKIES WITH AL CAPONE

■ ■

Thursday, May 28, 1936

When my father wakes me, he has his safety glasses on.

"Why are you wearing your shooting glasses?"

"Oh." He takes them off.

"Think you could miss a day of school?" he asks.

I pull myself up in bed, trying to keep the grin off my face. "Breaks my heart."

"No big tests or anything?"

I shake my head. "Nope."

"Good, because the strike is on. I need you to unload the laundry from the early boat and pack it in the back of the truck." He squints at me. "It's normally a six-man job. Do you think Piper would be of any use to you?"

"Maybe."

My father heads for his room.

I slip my trousers on. I'm just buttoning my shirt when the escape siren rings and my father dashes out, the door banging behind him.

The escape siren? I thought the cons were refusing to leave the cell house, not breaking out. Must be to signal all the guards to report up top.

Out the window, I see Mr. Mattaman and Mr. Bomini

fly by. Thundering footsteps shake the floor. The Nose sticks his arms in the sleeves of his jacket and half runs across the dock. An officer who lives in #1H leaps into the back of the pickup, and Darby Trixle guns the truck up the hill.

This sure beats school!

Down at the dock, I'm waiting for the military boat to pull in when Piper appears. I'm glad to see her, but not in a boyfriend kind of way.

"Your dad said you needed help."

"Uh-huh. What's happening up there?" I ask.

"Every one of them stayed in their cells except Fastball. If he strikes, he won't get probation."

"Easy choice."

She crosses her arms. "No, it's not. The other cons will beat him to a bloody nub for not striking. And if he fights back, he'll get written up for that."

"That's not fair!"

"How many times do I have to tell you, Moose—prison is not fair," she says as the boat officer unhooks the rope and we step on board. Our prisoners do the washing for the military bases on Angel Island, Fort Cronkite, and a few others. There is a ton of laundry. Who will do it now?

The laundry bags are heavy as dead bodies and just as awkward to carry. Not that I've ever carried a dead body, but still.

"My dad says it's unusual for them to work together like this. Usually it's every man for himself. He thinks Capone is behind it," Piper says.

"What's Capone want?"

"At his old prison he had booze and a radio in his cell. He's a big talker, so he doesn't care for the rule of silence, either."

"He's never going to get that lifted."

"Not with my dad in charge," Piper says.

Back and forth I go, tossing bags onto the dock until my shoulders ache and my pits are wet with sweat. Piper carries one bag for my three, but still, it helps.

The boat officer looks at his watch and then scans the remaining pile. He takes his jacket off and pitches in to help us.

With each trip back onto the boat, I scan the switchback, hoping to see my father. I'm proud that he's asked me to do a real job. I bet I'm the only guy at school who's ever worked all day at a prison.

When we're finally done, we head up top to let them know we need the truck.

Outside the warden's house, we see Fastball sweeping the front stoop and Bug batting the broom. Fastball slows the broom, and Bug creeps after it. He sweeps faster, and she leaps for the bristles.

"Hey, Moose." Fastball waves me over. Piper hangs back.

Fastball picks up Bug and scratches her under her chin, which starts her purr motor going. "If something happens to me, will you take care of Bug?"

I want to say "Nothing is going to happen to you," but I don't know that. "Sure." I tighten my grip on my thumb.

How do I handle this? I'm just trying to figure it out when Piper waves to me, and I hurry back.

Down by the lower cell-house door, we spot the truck

and head for the cutoff. I'm about to call to my dad when I hear his voice—tense and agitated. He's talking to Warden Williams. We scoot behind the truck bed to listen.

"It's a reasonable request," my father says.

"Reasonable? Don't be naive" is the warden's gravelly response.

"Denying a reasonable request makes us unreasonable." My father again, struggling to stay calm.

The warden snorts. "They get hungry, they'll go back to work, and we'll shake down each and every cell. Capone's is first on my list. Then we'll reassign."

"They hate when we change their cells. That's all they have. That's home."

"We can't have them pulling stunts like this. They brought the entire prison to a grinding halt."

"There are other ways of handling this," Dad says.

"That's what you think with your, what . . . eighteen months of experience."

"Forgive me, sir, but—"

The warden turns and walks back to the main road, his back straight, his shoes shiny, and his hat snugly on his head.

My father hurries after him. "And what about Fastball? He did what we wanted, sir. We have to protect him."

"The seg cells are full. Get these guys back working, Cam. We're going to lose the laundry contracts, and it's putting us weeks behind in our mat orders."

The warden's jaw hardens when he sees Piper. She tries to talk to him, but he walks faster, as if he wants to lose her.

My father opens the hood of the pickup. "Moose." He

smiles at me, but his eyes are clouded. "I heard you were working hard down there."

I beam. "We finished up, but we need the truck," I say importantly.

"Just let me get it squared away here; then I'll send it down. When the nine o'clock comes in, could you unload the supplies?"

"Yes, sir," I say.

"You play ball around four, don't you? Knock off for that, but take Natalie with you. Your mother needs a break."

My mother needs a break? I guess she's still upset. Last night, my father said, "Natalie's birthday is always a hard day for your mom. Give her time. She'll snap out of it."

I nod and act like it isn't the least bit weird for a high school guy to take his big sister to baseball practice. This isn't the time to give my dad grief.

I'll get Nat set up with her buttons in the shade of a tree, and hardly anyone will notice she's there. I've done it before.

I just hope I don't have to deal with Piper. She spent half the day with me. Isn't that enough?

I'm carrying the last crate of tomato sauce cans to the canteen when Bea Trixle shouts: "Phone, Moose!"

When you get a call during prime time, you've got to run like you're stealing bases to get there before the operator gives up on you, or someone on the island hangs the phone back on its hook so they won't miss their call.

Across the way, the phone swings on its cord. "Moose." Scout's voice is patchy with static.

"Aren't you at school?" I ask.

"Came home for lunch. What's your excuse?"

"Prisoners are on strike."

"Oh. Nice one!"

"Yeah, except I got to do all their work."

"Oh, sorry. Well anyway, did you get it?"

"Get what?"

"The photo of you and Capone."

"Like I said, Scout, that's never going to happen. For one thing, we don't own a camera."

"You can borrow my dad's Brownie."

"Scout, listen to me. Al Capone is locked up in a high-security prison, and I'm not allowed inside. It's not like I have milk and cookies with him. You've been to Alcatraz. You know how it works."

"Yeah, but Beck wants a photo."

I snort. "And I want to play ball with Babe Ruth."

"How else are we going to get on the team? We can't go back to our old one. They invited a bunch of fifth graders who throw like girls."

"How 'bout we talk to Passerini? He likes us."

"He's not the captain."

"He knows Beck. He'll know what to say to convince him to let us play."

"Worth a try." Scout's voice breaks up. "You're coming, right?"

"With Natalie."

"Yeah, okay. Four o'clock?"

"Four o'clock." I hang up the receiver.

* * *

When it's time to go, Nat is wearing Bea's dress, only in blue. Wait … there are two of them? "Where'd you get that?" I ask.

"Bea."

"She bought you two identical dresses?"

Nat doesn't answer.

I sigh. "Well, you can't wear your new dress or your new shoes," I inform her. "They're for church."

"Not for church," she mutters, staring at herself in the mirror in our parents' room.

She's right about that. It sticks to her girl parts too much for church. "Okay, but we're going to the baseball field. That's not where you wear an outfit like that."

She wraps her arms around herself. "Bea's gift."

I glance at the clock. "Save it for another time. You don't want to get it dirty."

Nat stands there, her lips stretching in all directions like she's tasting the different parts of her mouth.

The minutes tick by. If we miss the ferry, Scout's not going to wait for us.

"How about if you wear a coat?"

"Too hot," she says.

She's right, it is too hot.

"You can't walk in those shoes."

"Can walk in them," she says, her voice stiff and staccato.

Where is Mom? I could really use some help right now. But if I ask her, she might tell me not to go.

"They aren't comfortable. You never wear things that aren't comfortable!" I tell her.

"They are perfect with it." Natalie does a good imitation of Bea.

I look at the clock. We have two minutes to make it down there.

"Nat, please!"

"Roll with the punches. The punches. Roll with the punches," Nat mutters.

She's telling *me* to roll with the punches. The nerve of her. I throw my hands up. "Wear what you want. Let's go."

9. DEAD FLY PILE

■ ■

Thursday, May 28, 1936

When we get to Scout's apartment, he's sitting on the top of the icebox. His little sisters are pretending to be soldiers with stick rifles, marching back and forth in front of him.

Scout salutes. "Prisoner seeking permission to leave the house."

The smaller sister giggles, her curly hair jiggling. The older one with the ponytail keeps her stern officer's face. "Permission granted," she chirps, and Scout slides off the icebox and runs to his room to get his ball bag. Scout's kitchen is jam-packed with stacks of clean dishes, jars of peaches, canisters of flour, and pans on shelves with curtains instead of cupboard doors.

"What's wrong with her?" The little one with the round arms and dimpled cheeks points at Nat.

I look back at Natalie, who is holding her arms tightly around herself.

"Nothing," I say.

The little one beckons with her finger. I lean down. "That's a lie," she whispers.

I shrug at her.

She nods hard.

I kneel down to her level. "She's magic," I explain.

"Ohhhh." The little girl's eyes grow large.

When Scout comes back into the kitchen, his bag is bobbling against his leg.

"Hey." He stops in his tracks when he sees Natalie. "Why's she dressed like that?"

"Talk to her, not me," I tell him.

His eyes swivel from me to her and back again. "Natalie." He backs against the curtain cupboard. "You look sooo . . ." He stumbles on the next word: "Nice. The blue is pretty."

Natalie smiles down at the rough-hewn wooden floor.

"Where's she going?" he whispers, and then catches himself. "Where are you going all dolled up like that, Natalie?"

"Baseball park."

He frowns and glances sideways at me.

"It's okay," the little one announces, skipping behind us as we head for the door. "She's magic."

Outside, on the sidewalk, pigeons scatter, half running in their weird, bobble-headed way. A short man with a long beard threads through a small crowd of people. I hurry to keep up with Scout.

"Any idea how we should do this?" he asks.

"Let's get Beck alone."

Scout stops suddenly, and Nat and I nearly ram into him. "A gun will get us on for sure."

"A gun?" I snort. "What are you, nuts?"

Nat holds herself tight. She doesn't like unplanned touches.

"Well . . . it would." Scout starts walking again. "Beck says if you don't have a photograph, you're lying about knowing Capone."

"Everybody knows Capone's in prison on Alcatraz, but that doesn't mean kids ever see him."

I look back at Natalie, her eyes intent on the ground, counting cracks in the sidewalk. She's doing better in her shoes, but she's still slow. We have to wait for her every block or so.

At the park, I get Nat settled, my eye on what looks like a pretty serious game. Dewey is hunkered down at third. Passerini is in the pitcher's hole. They don't exactly have a mound. Beck is at first.

"Hey, Beck." Scout waves to him as we climb up on the bleachers.

Beck takes off his cap, slicks his hair back, and puts the cap back on his head.

"What's the score?" I ask a kid with big ears and a fresh haircut.

"Seven–zero. Southy's killing them."

Scout and I exchange a look. This is not what we were expecting.

Passerini's pitches are slow and steady. He throws a meatball over the plate. The Southy guy smacks it hard, and the ball flies to Beck. Should be an easy out, but Beck fumbles, and now the bases are loaded.

Passerini's ears are red. His mouth is tight. He digs with his foot.

"Come on, Pass," I shout. "Give him what you got!"

Passerini throws another pitch, slow and low.

"Ball," the Southy hitter calls.

Looked like a strike to me, but I'm not behind the plate.

Next pitch the Southy guy smacks so hard, it flies over a parked car into the street.

Southy earns four more runs before Beck's team manages to put together three outs.

Dewey's up first. He holds his bat high, like he knows what he's doing. But first pitch, he swings early.

"Strike one."

Second pitch, he stands like a goon, watching the ball fly by.

"Come on, Dewey!" I shout.

Dewey's jumping around on the plate, like he can't wait to get at it. It's a ball, and he swings.

Scout groans.

Now Passerini is up. The pitch comes in slow and sweet. It makes my mouth water just watching it. Pass smacks it hard, and it flies toward second. The second baseman sees it. I'm sure it's going to sail over his head, but he leaps out of his shoes and snaps it into his glove.

Unbelievable.

Beck's up next. They must know he's good, because the pitcher walks him. But then a red-haired guy comes up and hits a foul ball, which the catcher gets in his mitt.

Worst inning I've ever seen.

Back in the field, Dewey fumbles a pop fly. Passerini walks two players. Beck trips and falls on his face. He spits out a mouthful of dirt.

They're way better than this. Sometimes slumps are like a

bad case of chicken pox. The pain has to run its course. You can't just snap your fingers and make it go away.

"Scout . . ." I run my hand along the painted bleacher. "Think they're going to want us watching this?"

Scout rips at his thumbnail with his teeth. "If they pull off a comeback."

"What are the chances?"

Scout wipes his mouth. "Not good. We could help, but they won't give us a chance." He sighs.

"I know," I say. We try to catch Beck's eye. He looks the other way.

We take the hint, gather up Nat, and head across the way to an empty field. Natalie gets settled under another tree, setting up her buttons in exactly the same way she did before. We pool our change, and Scout runs to the store for a pop.

He buys vanilla soda. It's a sweet, cold, fizzy burst in my mouth. I hand it back to Scout. "Leave some for Nat."

I know better than to give her any until the end. She doesn't share well.

Scout wipes his mouth and hands the last third to Nat. "I wish they'd give us a chance."

"After that game, they've got to," I say. We go back to playing catch.

By the time we return to the baseball diamond, the game is over, and most of the guys are gone. Just Beck, Passerini, and Dewey are splayed out on a patch of grass. Nat sits on the bleacher, and then Scout and I head over to the grass with Beck and them.

Beck is smacking flies with the palm of his hand and

putting the dead ones in a little pile. Passerini's legs are criss-crossed. Dewey's legs are kicked out in front of him. Pass and Dewey roll the ball back and forth between them.

No need to ask how the game turned out. It's written all over their faces.

Beck looks up when we sit down, and then back to his dead fly pile. "Who's that?"

I turn around. No one is behind us.

Beck drops a newly swatted fly in the pile. "That girl in the bleachers. The one decked out to kill."

My stomach twists. "That's my sister."

"What's she doing?" Beck asks.

"She has a button collection. She's"—my voice dies in my throat—"organizing it. Leave her alone."

Beck shakes his head. "That's not what she's doing."

I turn all the way around and really look. Natalie is running her hands over her hair. Her lips are puckered up, and she's making smacking sounds.

"Who's she kissing?" Beck asks.

"Got to be Passerini," Dewey snorts. "All the girls love him."

The guys laugh.

My cheeks turn burning hot. I jump up and dash to the bleachers. "Natalie, stop doing that!" I growl.

"Passerini! Passerini!" Beck calls.

"Go on, Pass . . . kiss her!" Dewey hoots.

"Hey, Pass. She wants *you*, Pass!" Dewey, Beck, and Scout are all laughing.

"Stop it, Natalie!" I hiss.

She quits smacking, but her lips remain puckered like they're frozen there. Her arms cover her ears, blocking me out.

I grab her hand. I know she hates this, but I can't stop myself. "Don't do that with your lips!" My breath is hot in her face.

Natalie wraps her arms more tightly around her head, covering her face with her elbows. She doubles over, rolls up into the footrest of the bleachers.

"They're making fun of you. Don't you see?"

But the more I talk, the tighter Natalie pulls inside herself.

I glance back at the guys. They aren't laughing anymore. They're staring. Even Scout.

"Get out of here!" I shout, rushing at them.

Then I head back to Natalie, pulling the hem of her new blue dress down where it has crept up, revealing her panties. "Nat," I say as gently as I can. "Let's go home."

But Natalie doesn't move.

Beck, Dewey, Passerini, and Scout leave.

The cooler evening air breaks up the afternoon heat. The sky gets blue-gray and then orange. The ghost of a moon peeks out.

Tramps and hobos arrive with their spoons and pans tied to their belts. At night the city is full of them. Nobody likes sleeping in the Hoovervilles outside town. Too much crime. We're lucky our father has a job.

The smell of burning wood and burbling stew makes me hungry.

"C'mon, Mom and Dad will worry," I say.

On the street behind us, horns toot, bicycles squeak. An old man shouts the headlines, peddling the evening news.

Finally, Nat opens her mouth. "Not going home with you," she mumbles.

"I'm sorry. I shouldn't have yelled at you. Please, let's go."

I watch her rib cage rise and fall. "No," she mumbles. "Passerini. Hey, Pass. Passerini, Passerini."

"He's gone, Natalie. They're all gone. Mom and Dad will worry. We have to go home."

I start walking, slowly, so slowly, hoping she'll follow.

She doesn't. I circle back and wait.

Finally, she uncurls herself from the bleachers and walks across the grass to me.

"Hey, Pass, Passerini, Passerini," she mutters as we walk to Fort Mason.

On the ferry trip to Alcatraz, across the gangplank, through the metal detector, and up the stairs of 64 Building. "Hey, Pass, Passerini, Passerini," she says.

10. WHAT IN THE WORLD IS A PASSERINI?

■ ■

Friday, May 29, 1936

The next morning when I wake up, Natalie is peering down at me.

I look out at the dawn light. "What time is it?"

She shakes her head wildly.

What is the matter with me? This is not what I'm supposed to say.

"Sun come up okay, Natalie?" I ask.

Her head stops shaking. She never answers the question about whether the sun comes up, but she gets upset if I don't ask.

"Baseball." She rocks from foot to foot. "Passerini, baseball. Passerini, Passerini."

I rip my pillow out and place it over my head.

"Hey, Pass, Passerini, Passerini," she says.

I crush my face into the mattress. This reminds me of when Natalie liked a convict: Alcatraz 105. It happened when we first came to the island. I was looking for a convict baseball. They're really hard to find because all con games are played inside the rec yard. And one of the rules for baseball on Alcatraz is it's an automatic out if a player hits a ball over the wall. One day Nat and me were searching on the west side, and I let her out of my sight. When I got back, there she was with the one convict who is allowed to walk around the island without a guard: the gardener. After that all she could talk about was the gardener, prisoner #105.

When I get up, Natalie is gone, and my father is in the kitchen drinking coffee. "Dad, do you need me today?" I ask hopefully.

He turns the page of his newspaper. "I don't want you to miss another day of school."

"It's fine, we aren't doing anything."

My father's jaw is set. He shakes his head. "I wouldn't feel good about that."

Great. School is the last place I want to go right now. I never want to see Scout again. How could he have laughed at Natalie?

On the way down to the dock, I imagine Scout playing with Beck's team in the fall. Of course he gets on and I don't. I'll be there in the stands, trying to keep Natalie from making kissing noises.

Should I chew Scout out? Ignore him? Pretend I'm not upset? I know my father would say I should talk to him about what happened. But that's too hard.

Maybe Scout won't come to school. Maybe I won't go to class. But when I walk into U.S. history, there he is, slumped down in the wooden seat with two inkwells in front of him. Scout likes two of everything. He likes having a spare.

My nails carve grooves in my palms as I walk by the chalkboard, where a kid is clapping erasers. The chalk in the air makes me sneeze.

"Moose," Scout mumbles when I slip into my seat. His eyes don't meet mine. "You finish your paper?"

My desk lid creaks as I lift it open to get a pencil. "Yep."

His eyes are on the flag, the teacher's desk, the wall maps, everywhere but on me. "Look, I'm sorry, okay? I didn't mean to laugh. It just came out. The guys always kid Pass about how all the girls loved him, and . . ."

My face burns blisteringly hot.

"Look, I talked to Beck and them. I told them they can't laugh at her. Only . . ." Scout's voice drops. "Could you tell her not to do those kisses and stuff?"

I work my pencil lead into the side of my desk.

Scout leans in. "Passerini didn't laugh at her. In case you didn't notice. He really is nice."

I press harder, popping the lead out of my pencil. "Did you get on the team?" My voice comes out in a hot rush.

"No, Beck's waiting for your photo with Capone."

"That's never gonna happen."

Scout's eyebrows slide up his forehead; he cocks his head and fixes me with a look. "You always say you can't do stuff, and then you figure out how."

"No, I don't."

"Yeah, you do. Remember the convict baseball?"

"I didn't give that to you, Piper did." I duck down under my table to get the popped pencil lead. I work it back into the headless cave at the top of the pencil.

"You got it. She gave it to me."

Okay, he's right about that.

"Scout, listen . . . I can't get a photo any more than I can hand Beck a million dollars. Did you talk to Passerini?"

"Yup. He said there's nothing he can do. Beck is pig-headed about not letting freshmen on. But he said they're playing tomorrow, and if we show up early and they need guys, maybe we'll get a chance."

"We will or you will?"

"Both of us. Look, I'm sorry, okay? Is that coming through that thick skull of yours?"

My lips smile without my permission. Pretty soon the rest of me is smiling, too. "Yeah," I say, "it is."

The bell rings, and Mrs. Mahoney, the teacher everyone has a crush on, floats in. All eyes are on her.

Scout taps on my sleeve. "Should I apologize to Natalie?"

I sink back into my hard wooden seat. "Yes," I say.

When I get off the ferry after school, Bea is talking to Officer Bomini. "I wish you would put a word in to Cam about Darby. You know he's not one to toot his own horn."

Officer Bomini nods politely.

Jimmy is unloading burlap sacks of flour and sugar onto the truck. I drop my stuff to help. Usually the dock convicts unload, but since they're on strike, it's just us. I never realized how much work the prisoners do.

I've just finished carrying a crate of oranges when Natalie appears. Where did she come from, and what is she doing out here by herself?

Bea rushes over in her high heels. "Oh my word, Natalie. What did you do to your hair?"

Nat's hair is flat on one side, sticking up on the other. Her bow clip is hanging by two hairs.

"Come here, dear." Bea fishes a comb out of her pocket and motions for Natalie to follow her.

I think there's no chance Nat will do this, but once again she surprises me.

"Friend," Nat mutters, following Bea to her apartment.

Oh great . . . Nat thinks Bea is her friend.

When they come back down, Natalie's hair is freshly combed, with a new green ribbon in it, and the truck bed is packed full of crates of fruit, big bags of flour, containers of eggs and syrup.

"What in the world is a Passerini?" Bea asks. "Some kind of cooking utensil?"

My face gets hot. "No," I mutter.

Bea squints at me. "Well, what is it, then?"

I try to change the subject. "Thanks for the, uh, um, hair ribbon or whatever," I mumble.

"A boy. A boy. A boy," Natalie says, her fingers flapping, her eyes looking into the late-afternoon light.

Bea stands up straight. "Passerini is a boy? Natalie has a fella. Well, isn't that the bee's knees. I don't suppose you have a photograph of your young man?"

"She doesn't," I snap. "Natalie, let's go."

Bea click-clacks after us. "How'd she meet this Passerini fella?"

I'm trying my best to hurry Natalie up the stairs just as my mother comes running down, one shoe on, one shoe off, and her sweater on backward. "Natalie, for goodness' sake! You're not supposed to go down here by yourself!"

"Oh now, Helen! Give her a little freedom," Bea calls up

from the first stair. "Your girl is growing up. She has a fella and everything."

My mother's face falls. Her back stiffens.

"My Janet isn't old enough for boys, but I can't wait until she is." Bea says.

"Natalie isn't interested in boys," my mother barks.

Bea winks at me. "Mamas are the last to know."

My mother's eyes grow smaller. Her lips disappear. "Excuse me?"

"Oh, Helen . . . you've been dressing her like an overgrown ten-year-old, and you know it. You want her to look like all the other young girls, don't you?" Bea makes no attempt to get closer. She seems happy to shout this information for all the world to hear.

My mother runs down past us to Bea. For a second I think she might punch her. She steps right up close to Bea's face. "No."

"Oh, you can't mean that. You don't want her to stand out like a sore thumb. All she'll get is *pity*, Helen. From where I sit that young lady of yours should have a chance at happiness, yes indeed. And, Helen. You might want to put your sweater on the right way."

My mother's lip trembles. Her face turns as gray as an old baseball. She turns and runs up the stairs to us, her shoulders pitched forward like she's pushing through heavy wind.

When we get inside our place, she closes the front door and leans her whole weight against it.

"Change out of that dress. You're not to wear it again," my mother commands.

Natalie heads for the kitchen and begins throwing open

cupboard doors. She pulls over a chair and climbs up to check the top of the icebox.

"Natalie, did you hear me? I mean now!" my mother shouts.

"Cake." Natalie opens the oven door and then bangs it closed.

"After you change."

"Cake." Natalie begins to spin.

"Change out of that dress, and I'll cut you a piece." Mom's voice quavers.

Natalie hugs herself tightly as she whirls around.

"Come on, sweetie." My mother tries to fake-wheedle her.

"Cake, cake, cake!" Nat's hands catch the air as she spins.

"Natalie, what about that new dress I got you? It's made of that soft fabric you like so well. Put that on and you'll get your cake."

"No little girl dress. No." She turns faster.

My mother marches to Nat's closet and pulls the pink dress off the hanger. She unbuttons it, walks back to the kitchen, and shoves it in Natalie's spinning face. "Take that dress off. It makes you look—"

Natalie hugs herself.

"Natalie, now!" my mother shouts. It's awful when my mother loses control. Then it seems like there are two Natalies.

"No now! No now!" Natalie knocks a vase off the shelf. It falls with a thud. A glass bowl crashes, splintering into pieces. She bangs her head against the wall, bites at her wrists, kicks the books off the shelf, and then collapses in a heap in the middle of the broken shards.

My mother is shaking hard. She stands next to Natalie, unable to move.

11. No Kissing Noises

Saturday, May 30, 1936

In the morning when I wake up, my father is gone, and my mother is dressed for work, her music bag slung over her shoulder. She doesn't say a word about yesterday. She doesn't ask me what I'm going to do with Natalie today. She just sweeps out the door like she's making a dash for freedom.

I pull open all my drawers, but convicts on strike means no clean clothes. I dig a shirt out of the dirty-laundry bag.

Natalie toe-walks across the living room, where I'm sitting with my legs kicked over the couch arm, eating Natalie's cake and reading about the Babe. Stale birthday cake is a little-known breakfast delicacy, and there's no fact about the Babe I don't want to know. I love what he says. Like this, for example: "You stand there at the plate watching the pitcher wind up. You haven't a way in the world of knowing what he is going to serve you, and it is not much use trying to guess because a good hurler can disguise his wind-up so that you get a fast one when you think a curveball is coming."

Natalie stands so close to my chair, I can smell her breath. "Baseball," she says.

I take another bite of cake. "We're not doing that."

"Hey, Pass, Passerini," Natalie says.

"All the girls like him, so get in line," I tell her.

"Natalie, Natalie, Natalie . . . I do," she mutters.

"I know you do. You've made that all too clear." I stumble into the bathroom. She follows me to the doorway. I turn on her. "You can't go around pretending to kiss people. You'll get made fun of. Now do you mind?" She steps back, and I shut the door.

When I finish my business and peek out, she's still standing there.

"If you like someone, you have to pretend you don't," I tell her.

How do you explain pretending? Nat doesn't pretend. She's the most matter-of-fact person in the world.

"I know it doesn't make sense, but that's the rule." I head into the kitchen. "You have to act like you don't like Passerini."

I grab a piece of paper and start writing.

The Rules
1. Do not pucker your lips.
2. Do not make kissing noises.
3. Do not stare at Passerini.
4. Do not wear your Bea Trixle dress.
5. Always do what I say.

I stick the page in her face. "We'll go to the park to watch baseball so long as you follow these rules."

Natalie nicks at her collarbone with her chin. "Follow these rules," she parrots.

I watch her carefully. "Say 'I understand.' Say 'I will follow these rules.'"

"Moose's rules."

"Yeah, they're my rules for you."

"Moose's rules for Moose."

"What?"

"Moose's rules for himself." She tries again.

"Oh . . . you want rules for me? Let's see. . . . Be careful of Piper. Don't throw any baseballs through any windows. Remember when I did that? It took me a whole year to pay Mom and Dad back."

She wrinkles her nose like she's smelling something stinky. "Piper, Annie, Piper, Annie rules," she mutters.

I stare at her. The elastic in the cuff of her flannel pajamas has been removed. She couldn't stand how tight it was. The corner of her mouth has yellow in it. Egg yolk, probably. But her hair shines with whatever Bea put on it. Her skin is clear. She has never even had one pimple. I look into her big green eyes, which look everywhere but at me.

"You want to know my rules about Piper and Annie?"

"Piper and Annie rules," Nat mumbles.

"I've had a hard time figuring that out." I peer at her. "Turns out having a girlfriend is complicated. I can't trust Piper, and Annie, well . . . it's too hard to be the boyfriend of somebody you know that well."

"Mommy and Daddy," she says.

My eyebrows slide up my face. "You want to know Mommy and Daddy's rules? How should I know?" I stare at her.

"Mommy and Daddy know too well."

"Oh." I nod. "You're right. They do know each other really

well. But I'm not even fourteen yet. I'm not ready to have a girlfriend."

"Not ready."

I groan. "You want to know what that means? I wanted to spend time with Jimmy and Scout without Annie around, and that hurt her feelings. I didn't want to hurt her feelings, but I didn't want to spend all my time with her, either. It was too hard."

Natalie's eyes seem to be taking this in. Sometimes telling things to Natalie is easier than telling them to anyone else. She doesn't make suggestions about what I should do. She just listens.

When it's time to go, she has the green dress on again.

I grab the page and shake it in her face. "Rule number four. You can't wear Bea's dress. I'm not taking you if you wear that."

Natalie rocks on her feet. She bites at her lip like she's trying to get something off it.

I plunk myself on the couch and fold my arms. She disappears into her room and comes out with the other Bea dress, in blue.

I march into her room and fling open her closet door and stare into the dark, empty space. The only other dress hanging in there is the green one.

"Where are all your dresses?"

"Bea Trixle."

"Bea took your dresses?"

Nat shakes her head. "Natalie gave . . . I gave. I did."

"*You* gave them to Bea?"

Man, I can't believe this. Why can't this be somebody else's life?

Natalie doesn't answer, but I can tell by the way she's twisting her lips with her fingers that I'm right.

"How come Bea got you two dresses?"

Nat wrinkles her nose. Her eye twitches. "Hers," she says.

Of course. They were hers. That makes sense. They wouldn't fit her now, but she must have been able to wear them once. "Does Mom know?"

Nat cocks her head like she has a toothache.

"I guess not. Okay, okay, but no kissing noises. Swear to me." I point at her.

"No kissing noises, swear," she repeats.

"You know what kissing noises are, right?"

She puckers her lips and gives the air a big fat smackeroo.

"Yep, you do."

Natalie picks up her handbag with the buttons inside and follows me out the door.

The sun is bright, glistening white on the water, and the sky is blue. A flotilla of sailboats moves in a crooked line, and a big ferryboat toots its horn.

Piper is standing on the dock in front of the *Coxe* in her white shoes, white shirt, and blue pearl-button sweater, a book bag hooked over her shoulder.

I love the way she smiles like she's been waiting for me. Wait, no, I don't. I don't like anything about her.

"Bea said to give this to you, Nat." She hands Natalie a postcard.

Natalie reads it. Takes it up close to her eye like she's checking it for authenticity, then gives it to me.

May 28, 1936

Dear Natalie,
    Remember what you told me. You are a young lady, and you want to learn how to act like one. I'm proud of how far you've come.
    I'm having a great time with my brother, though he doesn't take direction as well as you do. Be home soon.

Yours truly,
Mrs. Carrie Kelly

"Thanks for bringing her the postcard," I say.

"Sure. I'm not working today. Mother said I should stick with you. Your father told me you were going into the city."

The dock officer pulls my card, Piper's and Natalie's. "Not today."

"Sure looks like you're going into the city."

"No, I mean . . . I'm going into the city, but you can't come along."

"You said you'd watch me, remember?" Piper follows us across the gangplank. "Besides, they already pulled my card."

"Okay, but you can't come with us," I call back to her.

"Well, I am," she announces.

I turn to face her. "It's . . ." I try to think of what my

mother says when someone wants to schedule a lesson when she isn't available. "Not a good time."

"Why not?"

"It just isn't."

"You're going to be playing, right? I can watch Natalie." Piper settles in next to me in the bow. She smells like lemons and new sneakers.

I step away from her and stare out at a dock piling that has been dive-bombed with white bird turds. "Look, not today, okay?"

"I'm already on the boat, Moose."

I toss an old piece of popcorn from my pocket into the water and watch it float away. "You can't come with us."

"My mom told me to stick with you. You don't want me to disobey her, do you?"

I search for more old popcorn. "Since when do you do what she says?"

I find an old piece of candy covered in pocket fuzz and toss that in the water.

"You know you want me to go," she says.

I groan and spin to face her. "You can be so annoying sometimes."

"Yeah," she laughs, "I know."

12. My Skull Is Melting

Saturday, May 30, 1936

Scout comes flying out of his apartment like he's been waiting for us and he wasn't entirely sure we'd come. "Piper." He smiles.

"Hi, Scout," she says.

"And, Nat"—he turns all his attention to her, then drops his voice low—"can I talk to you for a minute?"

Piper looks over at me, but I'm not about to explain. We watch Scout and Nat walk up to the neighbor's fence. We can't hear what they say, but Scout keeps wiping his palms on his pants, and Natalie rocks from foot to foot, cocking her head to the right.

A few minutes later, Scout motions for us to go.

"Everything okay?" I ask Natalie as we cross the street.

"Sad," she mutters. "Yesterday, sad."

I stare at her. "Yeah, I know."

We walk by a butcher shop with rows of pink chops and bright-red steaks in the window, and then a photographer's studio. Piper and I are walking together. Natalie is a few steps behind us. Scout runs ahead. He doesn't know how to walk.

I just get Nat caught up when Piper lags behind. "Piper, come on!" I shout.

I keep going, hoping she'll catch up, but when I look back, all I see is a sailor carrying a suitcase and a long line of fast-moving cars.

"Wait a second," I tell Scout and Nat, and double back for Piper.

Piper is staring in the window of the photographer's studio, which is full of formal photos: men in military uniforms, twin girls in matching dresses holding hands, and, smack in the middle: Warden Williams in his blue double-breasted suit, Mrs. Williams in a lace-collared dress, and baby Walty in a tiny sailor suit.

"Hey," I smile, "that's *your* family."

She tosses me a hateful look, pivots on her heel, and takes off, barely missing a policeman. I run after her. When she catches up with Scout and Natalie, she turns on me. "What are you looking at?" she growls.

Scout and I stare at each other.

What happened to her? She take a grumpy pill, or what? Just five minutes ago she was fine, and then she saw that sweet photo and ... oh ... the Williams family photo was missing one very important family member. Her.

I match my steps to hers. "You were away at boarding school."

"YOU THINK I DON'T KNOW THAT, MOOSE?" she barks, her eyes as hard as teeth.

Now what do I say? I feel bad for her. I wouldn't like seeing a family photo of my family without me. "Okay, I'm sorry," I mumble.

"I'm not upset. I'm not. So just shut up, okay?" Her face is a closed door.

What do I say to that? I have no idea.

Scout puts his fingers in his mouth and whistles. "C'mon! We have to get there early. It's our only chance to play."

I hurry to catch up.

We cut through a back alley to the baseball field, which is already packed full of guys. I scan the field until I spot Passerini warming up with Dewey.

"Natalie." My voice closes around her name. "Remember what you promised."

Piper's head pops up from her book bag. "What did she promise?"

"Nothing," I mutter.

Natalie shifts her weight from foot to foot.

Passerini looks over and sees Natalie. I drop my gear bag. "Please no smackeroo noises. Please, please, please."

My skin feels hot and itchy, as if hives are forming everywhere.

Why do I have to do this? I hate my parents sometimes.

Passerini motions to Dewey to wait and walks directly to us, his dark eyes uncertain, his skin a sunburned red. He looks Nat straight in the face.

"I'm sorry." Passerini bows. "I hope you'll forgive my friends."

Natalie melts like chocolate in the sun. "Passerini," she mumbles. "Passerini, Passerini."

He smiles. "Pleased to meet you, Natalie." He holds his hand out for her to shake.

Natalie doesn't take it.

Passerini glances at me for direction. He starts to pull his hand back when her hand darts out and shakes just his baby finger. But when the shake is done, she still holds on.

Passerini's mouth tightens. His eyes waver.

Oh great . . . there's no rule for this. "Let go," I say.

Nat lets go, and my breath comes out in a big burst.

Passerini recovers himself, gives another gentlemanly bow, and then reaches in his pocket. When he pulls his hand out, his fist is closed around something.

Passerini unfurls his fingers like a street performer. In his palm is a button.

Natalie gasps.

"It's for you . . . to make up for my stupid friends," he says.

It is so nice of him to do this, but I really wish he hadn't. Does he have any idea how crazy she is about him?

Nat takes the button tenderly, as if it were a quail egg.

She stares at the button. "Passerini, Passerini, thank you, Passerini."

"Sure," Passerini says, and runs back to the field with a long look at Piper.

"Ahhhhh, so that's who it is," Piper says. "Bea was telling me Natalie had a boyfriend. He's handsome, all right. She knows how to pick 'em."

"He's not her boyfriend."

Piper laughs in my face. I've never known anyone to enjoy my pain as much as she does.

"Could you and Nat just sit over there?" I point to the tree.

"Of course, Moose." She tosses me a mocking smile and heads for the shady tree.

"Moose," Nat says.

"Yeah," I say.

She has her fingers closed around the button. I think she wants to show me, but she unclasps her handbag and digs her hand in. Probably looking for the perfect place for Passerini's button.

"A gun will get us on for sure," she mumbles.

"What?"

And then I see her pull something big and silver out of her purse. My father's revolver.

My throat closes up. I can't swallow.

She dangles it upside down.

I gently take the gun from her. Dad's going to kill us. Kill me. Kill everyone. "How'd you get this?"

She doesn't answer.

"Why'd you bring it?"

"On the team. Moose on the team. Moose," she says.

Oh no . . . she brought it to help me.

I stick the gun back in her purse and cover it up with buttons.

"Hey, I saw that," Piper hisses.

"What?"

"The revolver."

"No, you didn't," I say.

Scout's footsteps pound up behind me. "Didn't you hear? Beck said we could play."

"I got it. I'll keep it safe." Piper winks at me.

"Keep what safe?" Scout sticks his nose between us.

"Don't worry," Piper tells me.

"What's going on?" Scout demands.

Piper fixes her eye on Scout. "Natalie brought a gun."

"WHAT?" Scout sputters, spit flying out of his mouth.

"Uh-huh. It's in her purse," Piper tells him.

Scout turns to Natalie. "May I see?" he asks.

"Leave it alone, Scout," I plead.

Natalie rolls from one foot to another. "Scout can see," she mumbles, smiling to herself.

I walk up close to Scout's face. "No!"

Scout dives for the bag. "I'm asking Natalie, not you."

My head feels hot. My skull is melting.

Scout opens the clasp, digs his fingers through the clicking, clattering buttons, and pulls out the shiny new revolver.

13. A Guy with a Purse

■ ■

Saturday, May 30, 1936

I snatch the gun from Scout. "We're going home." I fit the revolver back in Natalie's purse, grinding my teeth against the crush of disappointment. Beck said we could play, and now I have to go home.

Natalie ruins everything. I want to yell at her, but how can I? She did this for me.

Beck appears, his eyes shifting from me to Scout. "What's happening?"

"Natalie brought a gun so you'd put us on the team for permanent," Scout announces.

Beck's eyes light up like headlights.

"Shut up, Scout," I say.

"I didn't make her bring it, Moose, but now that she has . . ." Scout's voice trails off.

"Let's see," Beck demands.

"You might as well show him," Piper tells me.

I pull out the gun. What choice do I have?

Beck's eyes shine. "Is it real?"

Scout scowls. "Course it's real. Can't you tell?"

Since when did Scout become a firearms expert?

"Is it loaded?" Beck asks.

"Let's check." Piper takes the revolver, pushes a latch forward, turns the gun on its side, and empties the bullets into her palm.

Everyone stares at her like she's made a baseball float in the air. She just shrugs. "My father's been a warden my whole life. He's taught me a thing or two." She slips the bullets into her pocket.

"Let me see?" Beck's hand trembles.

"No!" I say.

"What can it hurt if it's not loaded?" Piper hands the gun to Beck.

Beck runs his finger along the inside rim. "Can I keep it?"

Scout steps forward. "We'll be on the team for sure, right?"

"You can't keep it. I have to take it back," I say.

Beck closes one eye, holds the gun up, and aims it.

My arms get itchy. I swipe at myself. "Give it back."

"How about if I take it," Piper says. "I'll make sure it's safe while you play. We'll put it up high in that tree. We can take it home when you're done."

"So, wait." Scout's voice is louder now. "Does this mean we're on the team, Beck?"

Beck shrugs. "Sure . . . if I get to keep it."

"Never happen," I say.

Beck tsks. "Too bad. I thought you wanted on the team."

Scout bulges his eyes at me.

Passerini is tossing a ball from hand to hand. "Hey, know what? I got to leave early. Could we play ball already?"

There are nods all around.

"Can't you put it away or something?" Passerini asks.

"Like I said, up in the tree," Piper says as a bunch of little kids run by.

I think this over. Really, what trouble can an empty gun cause hanging in a tree?

"Passerini." Nat says his name like it's a fancy pastry.

Beck snorts.

Passerini turns red. "I'll climb up," Scout offers. He shinnies up the tree. When he's partway up, I hand him the purse, and he scoots up farther, hooking the handbag on a branch. He scrambles down the trunk and leaps free, brushing off his pants.

Passerini keeps tossing the ball as he walks out to the field.

Beck picks up his glove. "You better be good," he tells us.

"Don't worry, we are," Scout says.

I pull on my glove and head for the field to warm up with Scout. We start right out tossing the ball back and forth at blistering speeds.

Beck is on the other side, throwing with Passerini. They're doing a normal warm-up. They don't have anything to prove.

My arm is sore by the time Beck calls, "Scout, catcher. Moose, right field."

Right field? Shoot. But I smile as if I want right field. Nobody likes a complainer.

Stay light on your feet, I tell myself. Watch the ball. Know your options.

I glance back at Natalie. Uh-oh, her buttons are up in the tree. I forgot about that. What's she going to do?

But she and Piper are walking across the field with books

on their heads. Piper is talking to Natalie and laughing. Weird.

The first half hour, Scout catches two foul balls, but nothing comes near me. Oh great . . . how will Beck see I can play if no ball comes out here?

When we are up, Beck puts both Scout and me at the end of the line. We don't even get a chance at bat before the team's out.

Headed to the field again, I try not to act disappointed.

"Moose, take first," Beck calls.

First base!

Instantly, I forgive Beck for everything he's ever done. First base is like wearing my old pajamas. So comfortable.

I stand, watching Passerini pitch.

A grounder skitters across the field between first and home. I cut it off. Get it in my glove, scoot back, and tag the guy out.

I grin, but not too big. It's only one out.

Next hit is a fly ball to left field. Runner makes it to my base, but then he gets greedy and goes for a steal. Passerini zips the ball to second. Beck sends it to me. I get it solidly in my glove. Out number two!

Passerini gives me an appreciative nod. My chest swells.

Next batter hits a pop fly. I run for it. Get underneath it. Then lose it, blinded by the sun. But it drops back into view, and I wrap my glove around it.

"Got it!" I wave my hand in the air.

Scout's eyes find mine. He's the only person who knows how much this means to me, because it means that much to him, too.

We head up to bat again. This time Beck puts Scout up first, then me.

Scout's leg is jittering the way it does when he gets nervous. This may be our only chance to show what we've got. I'm a steadier hitter than Scout is. But if Scout's having a good day, he can smack the ball like nobody's business.

I nod my encouragement.

He picks up the bat and walks out there.

When he pulls the bat back, his leg quiets, his eye tracks the ball in the pitcher's glove. The first pitch is wildly off.

"Ball," Beck calls.

Scout tips the ground and gets ready again.

The second pitch is smack over the plate. Scout swings and whacks it hard down center field, and takes off. The pitcher chases the ball, but nobody runs faster than Scout. He makes it with time to spare.

Wasn't one of Scout's best hits, but it will do. Now it's my turn.

When I pick up the bat, it feels too light. I get ready, trying to recalibrate my swing to the weight of the bat. The pitch flies at me. I swing too fast.

"Strike one," Beck calls.

Now my hands are wet gripping the bat. I wipe them on my pants and get ready again. The sun is in my eyes. The bat feels wrong.

Stay calm. Eye on the ball.

The pitch hurls over the left corner. Might be a ball. I hold.

"Strike two," Beck calls.

My arms are trembling. It looked like a ball, but it curved back in.

I steady myself. One more chance.

The ball comes at me solid. Watch it, watch it, swing. *Crack.* I get a piece of it. I drop the bat and run as the ball sails out to left field.

Left fielder has it. He spins it to first base.

I slide in just before the first baseman catches it.

Safe.

I wipe the sweat off my forehead. Now I just have to make sure I don't take a stupid risk.

The next batter hits a pop fly that the shortstop catches. Passerini is up next. First pitch he slugs the ball across the park. We all run in. Probably could have walked in—that's how great Passerini's hit was.

We win easily. Scout and I aren't the best players on the team, but we aren't the worst, either. We're in the middle of the pack. The high middle.

That's good enough, isn't it?

I sprawl out on the grass with the other guys—hot, tired, and happy. Scout is next to me. He looks up at the sky. "Anyone know what time it is?"

"Half past six," Dewey calls.

"Uh-oh." Scout jumps up. "Supposed to take my sisters to catechism."

He climbs up the tree, gets Nat's handbag, and then slides back down with the handle in his mouth. "See if Beck will let us play tomorrow," he whispers as he hands the purse off to me.

I glance back at Piper and Natalie, who has made pebble stacks around Piper's magazine.

Beck packs the base sacks into a bag. Dewey hoists the bag over his shoulder.

"Thanks for letting us play," I call.

Beck starts walking, doesn't look back.

"So . . . hey." I chase after him. "We're on the team, right?"

He ignores me.

I'm afraid to set Nat's handbag down, but what self-respecting guy carries a purse? "Beck," I call.

Dewey scurries back to me, lugging the heavy base bag. "Beck says you got to get him the picture of you and Capone, then you're in."

"Come on, Beck," I shout after him. "That's ridiculous."

Dewey glances at the purse. "Or he says the gun would do, too. But he needs it permanent."

"No," I say.

Dewey shrugs.

Beck watches from a distance. "You're not as good as you think you are, Moose!" he shouts.

I knead the inside of my cheek, hard. "We can play tomorrow, though, right?"

Beck turns away.

Dewey half runs to catch up with Beck, struggling under the weight of the base bag. He and Beck talk, then Dewey runs back. "Lot of guys," Dewey huffs, "want to play with us. You can play tomorrow if Beck feels like letting you."

I scratch a hive on my leg. This is wrong. We may be freshmen, but we're as good as the other guys.

It's still light out, but the air smells of paper burning. In the far corner of the field, a man with no shirt picks notes on a banjo; hoboes gather around a crackling fire.

I can't believe it's so late already. Baseball minutes go fast. Homework minutes go slow.

I gotta get that pistol back. I've never known my father to keep his gun at home. Normally, he locks it up at the firing range. I wonder what happened.

Natalie's pebbles are scattered on the grass. Luckily, she doesn't want to take them. Piper licks her finger and turns the page of her magazine.

"Time to go," I say, watching a bum with just one shoe walk by.

"Home now." Natalie gets up, her eyes glued to her feet. She starts walking, counting her steps.

I breathe in the smell of newly caught fish as we walk by a collection of blankets and bedrolls, crates and cardboard boxes.

"So, Piper . . ."

"Don't worry." She matches her step to mine. "I won't tell. You'll owe me, though."

I don't want to think what I'll owe her, but what choice do I have? "Thanks," I say.

At Fort Mason, we see the *Coxe* approaching. After the dock officer checks us off his list, Piper, Nat, and I get on. Boy, am I ready to go home. I'm hungry, and I have to pee.

On the boat, Piper drifts to the starboard side. Nat stays with me. I'm just staring at the approaching lighthouse on Alcatraz, the sun low in the sky, when suddenly I remember the metal detector. Everyone who comes onto the island has to walk through a metal detector. How are we going to get the gun back? A gun is what the metal detector is designed to detect.

I begin to sweat like I have a fever.

I could throw the gun into the bay. But what will my

father do when he can't find his gun? What will the warden do? You can't have a missing gun on a prison island.

I could hide it on the boat. But what if the boat officer finds it? They transport prisoners on this boat. . . . What if one of them gets a hold of it? No one will know it doesn't have bullets.

Everyone is standing in line by the door. The boat officer is fixing the rope to the cleat. Soon they'll open the rope barricade, and we'll file off.

That's when I see the canteen groceries. Crates of canned food. Tuna fish. Chicken noodle soup and pork and beans. Cans will make the metal detector go off. But they expect that.

My hands are shaking as I take out two rows of tuna and slip the gun underneath, then stack the cans over the top. Natalie stands by me, rocking gently.

The cans are uneven. I pull the gun out and remove another row. Still not flush, but better. You can't tell unless you really look. I stuff the extra tuna cans in a stack of old life preservers, and then I head out.

In the distance I spot Piper's mom and dad, waiting to get on the boat. They're all dressed up in evening clothes. Her mom is in a white fur coat. Her dad is wearing a tux. Piper heads directly to them, bypassing the metal detector. "Daddy! Mommy!" she calls, like she used to in the old days. I guess they've forgiven her. That's good.

I sure wish I could have bypassed the metal detector the way she did. But only Piper can get away with stuff like that. She's unbelievable. If I'd known she was going to do that, I could have had her carry the gun off. I hold my breath as I walk through, even though I know I don't have anything. Then I hang back while they bring the groceries through. My heart jolts when the detector goes off, but the boat officer glances down at the cans and looks no further.

My arms throb with relief. Once the crates are in the canteen, I'll find Jimmy, who has a key. The two of us will get the gun and put it back on my father's dresser, where I'm guessing Natalie found it.

Nat and me are headed for 64 Building when the dock officer approaches.

"Something you want to tell me, Moose?" he asks.

"Huh?" I mumble.

"It will go easier if you're honest," the dock officer says.

My mouth drops open.

"We got the bullets." He opens his hand to reveal six slim bullets. "Where's the gun?"

My neck swivels to Piper and her parents. Piper's face is buried in her father's chest. "I was so scared," she sobs. Piper's mom strokes Piper's hair. Her father mops at her cheeks with his handkerchief.

I hear a ringing in my ears. The world has gone hazy. My eyes are having a hard time focusing.

"In the tuna fish crates," I say, but I don't remember giving my mouth permission to speak.

He pivots on his heel and heads back to the boat.

Piper huddles with her parents, near the gangplank. Natalie picks at a sore on her arm. I stand in stunned silence.

When the dock officer comes off the boat, my father's gun is in his hand.

14. I Did Worse in My Day

■ ■

Saturday, May 30, 1936

Bo Bomini, my mom, Natalie, and me are shoehorned in the tiny dock office. Bomini and my mom are sitting on the two squeaky seats. Natalie is standing by the wall, her arms wrapped around herself. I'm in the two inches of floor between Natalie and the desk.

My mom stares at me. "Why in the name of Mary and Joseph would you touch your father's gun?"

What do I say? What kind of person snitches on a sister like Natalie? She brought the gun for me. She wanted to help me get on the team.

My lips press shut.

"Word is, this had something to do with the high school baseball team," Officer Bomini says. Bo Bomini has always liked me. I don't want him to think I did something this bad. He'll tell Annie, and what will she think?

My mom's eyes drill into me. "Is that true?"

"I want to be on the team," I mumble. This doesn't answer the question, but it's all I can think to say.

"As if we don't have enough problems, Moose." Her voice trembles.

"Unfortunately, I'm going to have to write this up. With

the strike, the BOP is watching everything we do. The warden wants to handle this himself, but he and the missus had a party to go to tonight. Gonna talk to you about it tomorrow. Probably better if Cam's around for that," Bo Bomini says.

"Of course," Mom says. "We appreciate your help, Bo."

Bomini's chair squeaks when he gets up. He pushes it out of the way and holds the door open with his back. My mom and I file out.

"No," Natalie says. "No, no, no." She rocks from foot to foot, unwilling to move forward.

She knows something isn't right.

"Let's go home, Nat," our mom says. But Nat won't budge.

I walk back in. "Nat, I know it doesn't exactly make sense, but it's better this way," I tell her as gently as I can.

She makes a grimace like she's taken a bite of horseradish. But she still doesn't move.

"You have to trust me on this," I whisper.

"Trust me on this," she repeats, following me out.

On the dock, with the bright light of the guard tower shining down, Officer Bomini tells my mother, "All boys are fascinated by guns. I did worse in my day, believe me."

Mom says nothing.

"High school. Tricky time. Wouldn't want to do it over again." He winks at my mother.

Natalie is ahead of us, toe-walking up the stairs. When we get to our apartment, she flicks the lights on and off, on and off.

With the door closed, my mother comes down like a hailstorm. "Criminy, Moose . . . what were you thinking?"

I could kill Piper for this. Why did she have to open her big mouth?

My mom peers at me.

I listen to the *click-click* of the clock, the pounding of Theresa Mattaman playing hopscotch on the balcony, and the *drip-drip* of the kitchen faucet.

My mother shakes her head, her eyes smoldering. "Don't you have anything to say for yourself?"

I stare down at the edge of the rug, which is beginning to unravel.

My mother waits.

Finally she turns away. "Make your own supper. I don't want to set eyes on you," she spits.

I count the hours until my father gets home, tiptoeing around my room like the floor is made of angel food cake. I sneak out to turn the radio on and then crack my door open enough to hear. I listen to one show after another, until just past midnight.

As soon as I hear his footsteps on the balcony, I burst out of my room. He smiles when he sees me and gives me a big hug. "What are you doing up so late?"

"Waiting for you."

His eyes register my distress. He frowns. "Let me change out of my uniform, and we'll have a piece of Mrs. Matta-man's pie and talk through whatever it is."

When he comes back, he has his old electrician's slacks on. "I put the pie in the oven. Tastes better warm. C'mon, it's a beautiful night. Let's go outside."

I follow him to the balcony. He leans against the railing, looking out at the dark water. The bay is shifting. You can see the line where two major currents meet. The sky is black and starless, with just a weird, flat-bottomed moon. A buoy *ding-ding-ding*s, and a rowboat whacks the dock. A single bird rides the water. He looks lonely with no other birds around.

My dad takes the scene in, then turns to me. "What's up?"

"I had a little problem, and I wasn't quite sure how to handle it. Did you hear about it?"

"Bomini said you had a rough afternoon. That's all I heard."

"You know how I'm trying to get on the high school team?"

He nods.

"Well, Beck, he's the captain. He's really interested in Alcatraz. They all are, but especially him. So Scout said, 'Why don't you bring in something that will, you know, impress him, and then he'll let us on the team?'"

My father reaches in his shirt pocket, pulls out a toothpick, and sticks it in his mouth. "Okay."

"So I said no."

He waits for more.

I look out at the vast, empty water. "Somehow your gun ended up at the park," I mumble.

"What?" He drops his toothpick. "Hold on a minute here. My gun?"

I'm not looking at him, but I can hear how hard he's breathing.

"No one got hurt, right?" His voice cracks.

"Right."

"Why in the world would you pull a chucklehead move like that?"

I don't answer.

"I'm assuming someone found out about this?"

"Yes, sir, the warden. He wants us both in his office tomorrow."

Dad's lips disappear into his mouth. His eyes look across the water to the lights of the East Bay.

"Do you understand how hard it's been with this strike?"

I nod miserably.

"I don't know what to say. I suppose we can be grateful Natalie had nothing to do with it."

My breath goes ragged. I open my mouth.

"I just can't help thinking you're better than this, Moose."

I trudge back into my room, each footstep more miserable than the last, and then I wait. Surely my father will knock on my door to give me pie. But he doesn't.

15. A Shriveled Heart

■ ■

Sunday, May 31, 1936

When I wake up, I don't want to get out of bed. It's the only place I feel like me and not that bad kid who took his father's gun.

Today I have to go up to the warden's and explain myself to him. How am I supposed to do that? I'd rather lose the World Series than tell the warden I did something I didn't do. Well, okay, maybe not that. But close.

My head throbs and my jaw aches. What if I tell the warden the truth, that it was Natalie? What if I don't tell him the truth? Will I have to live the rest of my life as the bad kid?

Why is it always so complicated? All I want to do is play ball and go to high school like a normal kid.

I grab my baseball bag and sneak out of my room without eating breakfast. I walk up to the parade grounds, which are empty and cool in the long morning shadows. On the bay a boat honks at a ferry. The ferry honks back. A flock of pelicans flies in the crisp blue sky. I throw the ball and catch it a few times. Then I toss it up and whack it with the bat. I hit one way and run the ball down, then hit back the other way.

I've just smacked a pretty good one, and I'm imagining Beck and them are watching, when Darby Trixle appears in a white shirt and gray slacks. He looks better than he normally does. His civilian clothes aren't as tight as his uniform.

"What you doing out here all by your lonesome, Moose?" Darby asks.

"Just playing around, sir," I say.

"You got a glove for me?"

"Excuse me, sir?"

"An extra glove. Let's see what you got."

I dig in my bag for my old glove and toss it to him.

"Give me a minute to get warmed up here. A little rusty, but I played my share of ball in my day." Darby slips on the glove, stretches his hamstrings, and jogs in place.

I look across the bay. The water sparkles in the trail of the sun. The sky is full of birds, and birds are swarming the water. Must be a fish run. I look back at Darby. "As soon as the strike is over, my dad will be around more."

"Sure thing," Darby agrees. "You know I've always liked your dad."

Actually, I didn't know that. I always thought he didn't like my dad.

I run back and toss him one. He catches it and zips it back.

He has a show-offy way of throwing, like he wants you to tell him how good he is every time he throws the ball.

"Get your bat and let me pitch you a few," he says.

"You were a pitcher?"

He catches it and throws it harder. "Don't believe me, huh?"

His pitches wobble at first, but when he gets warmed up, he does okay. Slow and steady and easy to hit.

I swing the bat back and smack it solidly. I'm grinning as I chase the ball down. If only Beck had seen that.

"So, you're going to high school in the fall, eh?"

"Yes, sir."

"You're looking grown up these days. Twice I 'bout mistook you for the Nose."

"Yes, sir," I say.

"You gonna play baseball in high school, I take it?"

I suck on the inside of my cheek. "Uh-huh."

"You play well. Shouldn't be much trouble getting on the team."

"Thanks," I mumble. All I want him to do is stop talking and pitch me another meatball. Nothing like the feel of slugging the ball high and hard.

But Darby slips my glove off and hands it to me. "Give my best to your dad. You tell him I'd be proud to be his number two man." He winks at me.

"Uh, sure," I say, though I don't know what he's talking about. My father is the number two man.

"Oh, and one more thing." He walks up close. "Tell him I'm keeping my eye on Fastball like he wants."

"Fastball, sir?"

He nods. "Your daddy's a sucker for a hard-luck story. None of them guys were locked up for singing too loud at church. But Cam says he's earned his chance and we got to make sure he gets it. The men up there are felons on the outside, not on the inside." Darby shakes his head. "That's what your daddy says, anyway.

"He's not going to make it up there without my help.

Remember what happened before. I stood by him, that's for sure," he says.

He's talking about when my father got stabbed. All Darby did was help carry my dad to the ferry, but to hear him tell it, he fought off fifteen convicts single-handedly. I try not to think about how pale my father looked that awful day.

"A lot of the men like my father. They respect him. He gets birthday gifts and Father's Day cards from them," I say.

I'll bet Darby Trixle never got a Father's Day card from a convict.

"If you want to be a good cop, you need a bad cop, is all I'm saying. You tell him I have his back."

"Sure," I say, but I will tell him no such thing. I try to put it all out of my mind as I head for the parade grounds, where Theresa and Jimmy are watching their baby brother, Rocky, play in the sand.

"Hey, what's going on?" Jimmy asks.

I sit down with a thud on the side of the sandbox and tell Jimmy and Theresa everything. When I get to the part about the gun, Theresa hops up. "What's going to happen to Natalie?" she asks.

"Nothing. Piper said it was me," I say.

"What's going to happen to you?" Jimmy asks.

I look out at all the birds in the distant water. Birds don't have to worry about anything except food. "I don't know."

Theresa plops down next to me. She stares hard with her big brown eyes. "You have to tell them the truth."

"I can't blame it on Natalie," I say.

"But it *was* Natalie," she says.

"Moose is right, Theresa," Jimmy insists. "Remember what happened with the fire? The second anything bad happens, they blame her, and everybody goes berserk."

I nod.

Theresa scuds the sand with her heel. "Why did Piper have to tell?"

"Because she's Piper," Jimmy says.

Theresa's lip puckers out. "It was none of her business."

"She's trying to get in good with her dad. She doesn't care about us." Jimmy helps Rocky carve a tunnel in the sand. "There's a rumor that your father is being considered for Warden Williams's job. Piper must know that."

I stare at Jimmy. "What?"

Jimmy lets the sand fall through his fingers. "I overheard the Nose and Bomini talking. The BOP doesn't like the way Warden Williams is handling the strike. Some people think this is all part of Capone's plan."

"Really?"

Jimmy nods.

I try to imagine my father as warden. He'd make a great warden, but would he be more of a target?

"That can't be right. My father hasn't been here that long."

"People like him. Bomini said he thought your dad could bring the island together."

"That's true," I say.

Jimmy goes back to digging. "I thought you'd be more excited about it."

"It's a lot to think about. Right now, I'm just trying to figure out how to get out of this mess. My dad and me are meeting with the warden later today."

"Did you tell your dad the truth?" Jimmy asks. Theresa's big brown eyes are taking this all in.

"I can't. If I do, he'll tell the warden, and everybody will get all upset and take it out on Natalie."

"I knew we shouldn't trust Piper. Her heart is black and all shriveled up," Theresa says.

Jimmy grins. "At least you won't have to watch Piper anymore, Moose. It might have been worth it, just to get rid of her."

16. THE RULES FOR BEING NATALIE'S BROTHER

■ ■

Sunday, May 31, 1936

I try to forget about the meeting with my dad and the warden, but I can't stop thinking about what Jimmy said. If my father were the warden, could I tell him the truth about what happened? If my father were the warden, would we live in the warden's house? If my father were the warden, what would happen to Natalie? And what would happen to him? Would he be more safe as the warden or less?

I distract myself by drawing diagrams of the field and thinking up different plays. I read my book about the Babe. I find an old piece of taffy and pick the wrapper off it.

My jaws are working the stale candy when I hear someone outside the door.

Must be Mom and Natalie coming home, or Jimmy or Theresa, or my father telling me it's time to talk to the warden. I jump off my bed and go into the living room, where I see Piper peering in the window. She's wearing a blue ribbon and a blue sweater, and her nose is pressed against the pane.

When she sees me, she crosses her arms. "I didn't mean to tell him."

I swing open the door. "Yes, you did. You swore to me you

wouldn't, and then the second you saw him, you shot your mouth off. . . ."

"I didn't swear. I just said. Saying is not swearing. And what was I supposed to do? I can't get in trouble or they'll send me away again. Anyway, I can fix it," she says, squeezing past me.

I prop open the door. "Get out."

"I didn't have a choice," she mumbles.

"Of course you did." My voice trembles.

"I'm the one on probation, Moose. The worst that can happen to you is you get bawled out."

I take a wobbly breath.

Piper sees her opening. She can read my face like a multiple-choice problem. "I could have said it was Natalie. I was protecting her. . . ."

"You want a prize for that?"

"No, but—"

"You said you wouldn't tell."

"The metal detector, Moose. They would have found it."

"I put it in the crate of tuna cans. They always make the metal detector go off. Nobody would have noticed the gun."

"I couldn't take that chance." Her eyes are intent on me.

"You got through with the bullets."

"I forgot I had them."

"Oh right . . . that's why you ran around the detector." I keep holding the door open, waiting for her to leave.

She snorts. "You know I'd get in so much more trouble than you would." She takes small, unwilling steps toward the door.

"Not everything is about you."

I slam the door behind her. A rush of air cools my sweaty forehead.

I have a headache and my skin itches. I raid the icebox and bring a box of crackers and a hunk of salami back to bed. I try to read, but not even facts about Babe Ruth stick.

It's almost four by the time my father gets home.

"You ready?" He looks me up and down. "Put on a clean shirt, comb your hair, and brush your teeth."

Brush my teeth? In the middle of the afternoon? Who does that?

When I get out of the bathroom, he walks around me. "Look, we both made a mistake. My gun should never have been here. We'll stand up and take our punishment like men."

"Could he fire you for this?"

"Yes, but I don't think he will."

I follow him across the balcony and up the stairs. There are leaves on the road, and scattered blobs of bird turd. The prisoners normally keep this road clean. When is the strike going to be over?

My father rings the warden's doorbell. Fastball opens the door, and Bug darts out. I chase after her, but she runs by me, doubles back, and tackles Fastball's foot. Fastball breaks into a grin.

"How are you holding up?" my father asks him.

"Fine, sir. It's when the strike's over we got to watch."

"Don't I know it." My father sighs.

On the way up the stairs to the warden's office, I ask my father, "Fastball will be okay, right? You'll make sure he's safe?"

"I'm trying," he says. "Not as easy as it sounds."

In the warden's office, we sit in the two large chairs. The clock ticks down the minutes. My father has a clipboard with him. He's writing a report on the strike. He's almost done by the time Warden Williams arrives.

The warden takes his time getting settled behind his desk. I think about my father sitting at that desk. He would make a good warden. Better than Warden Williams.

When the warden finally looks up, he says, "I'd like you to take me through what happened, Cam."

"On Thursday I was at target practice as usual. I've been working to improve my marksmanship on a variety of firearms. I'd just finished a round and was reloading when Bomini informed me the men on Broadway had refused to leave their cells. I ran down to the phone at Sixty-Four to call the control room. I wanted an accurate count of the prisoners involved.

"Officer Mattaman confirmed the strike had begun and told me it looked to be nearly one hundred percent. I called in to you, and you made the decision to ring the emergency bell.

"I believed there wasn't time to secure my firearm in the usual manner, so I made sure the safety was on and placed the gun on my closet shelf. Then I ran up top to answer the emergency call."

The warden fidgets with his desk pen. "Never a good idea to jettison procedure, but I recognize there were extenuating circumstances. All right then." The warden leans forward eagerly. Is he enjoying this? "I'd like you to explain what happened, Moose."

The hives are everywhere. I start scratching like mosquitoes are swarming me.

"Take me through how you discovered the gun was there. And what you did with it."

What do I say?

Adults always make it seem like there's a rulebook somewhere, and all you got to do is follow it. If Natalie has one, it's written in a language that hasn't been invented yet. And the rules for being Natalie's brother? Also indecipherable.

"Moose"—the warden narrows his eyes—"answer me."

"I made a mistake, sir," I mumble.

"A mistake? Is that all you have to say for yourself? You jeopardize the safety of everyone on and off the island, and you think you made a little mistake?"

"I see that's what you see, sir," I say in a quiet voice.

"Excuse me?" The warden's voice is sharp.

"Moose," my father barks.

My lips feel like two cement curbs butting up against each other. "I'm sorry, sir."

"Well." The warden fixes my father with a stern look. "I can't say that was heartfelt. I don't believe he realizes what he's done, Cam."

My father nods.

"I'm going to have to send Bomini's write-up to BOP, you know that, don't you, Cam? It isn't personal, I don't care what anyone says."

"Yes, sir," my father says.

"If he were my son, it would be a long time before he played baseball again."

What? What gives him the right to say that? That's just mean.

"I'd put him on the garbage run," the warden continues. "Give him a chance to reflect on his choices."

"I'm inclined to agree with you on that, sir," my father says.

I stare at my father, incredulous.

How could he say that? Boy, would I like to tell him the truth just to see the expression on his face.

My jaw clamps closed. I hold it in.

17. FRIEND OR FIEND?

■ ■

Sunday, May 31, 1936

The next thing I know, it's eight at night and my stomach is growling. If taking away baseball isn't bad enough, now they're starving me.

I tiptoe into the kitchen. The lights are off; nothing is bubbling on the stovetop or baking in the oven. Mrs. Mattaman is probably making lasagna or tortellini. My mouth waters just thinking about this.

I look in Natalie's room and the bathroom. Empty.

In my parents' room, Mom is curled up on her side of the bed, snoring softly, her head sunk into the pillow.

My dad must still be up at the cell house. But it's so late. . . . Where is Natalie?

Man, I hate when this happens. Doesn't anybody realize we live on a prison island?

I check her room again, open the door of the closet, look behind the bed, then run back to the kitchen.

This time I notice a note my mom left, anchored by the saltshaker. Why would Mom leave me a note when she's right here?

When I get closer I see it's not my mom's writing. It's Natalie's wobbly printing. Natalie wrote a note? That's a first.

At my fiend
Natalie

"Fiend"? She must mean "friend." Even so, this has never happened before. It's progress for Natalie, and I'd be happy, except where is she?

Who could her friend be?

Passerini. It's got to be him.

Please tell me Natalie doesn't know where he lives. She couldn't have found that out, could she?

I open my mouth to shout "Mom!" and wake her up. But what will my mom do? She'll head straight for Passerini's house and pound on his door. If anything could make things worse, it would be that. I've got to find Natalie myself. And I've got to do it now.

The dock officer will know if she got on the ferry, but they wouldn't let her walk on by herself, would they? Most officers know Natalie, but a new guy like the Nose?

If she took the ferry, her card will be in the OFF ISLAND slot. I'll check there first.

I run down the stairs to the dock office.

The lights are on. Officer Trixle looks up from his paperwork. "Moose." He frowns at me.

Why is he frowning? Does everyone on the whole island know I'm in trouble? Is this what it feels like to be the bad kid?

"Did Natalie get on the boat, sir?" I ask.

Officer Trixle glances at the cards. "Doesn't look like it." He shakes his head. "You folks ought to keep an eye on her. It's awful late. I saw her out with the birds earlier."

I let out my breath. At least she's not trying to hunt down Passerini, unless she snuck onto the ferry. She wouldn't do that, would she?

"Thank you, sir." I back out of there.

Okay, so who on this island does Nat think is her friend? Theresa Mattaman.

I run upstairs and burst through the Mattamans' door without knocking like I always do. Mrs. Mattaman looks up with a start. She's sitting at the table, writing a letter. Rocky is asleep on a blanket on the floor, his bottom straight up in the air. The apartment smells like garlic bread.

"Shhh!" She puts her finger to her lips.

"Is Nat here?" I whisper.

"No, dear," Mrs. Mattaman says as the bottle-cap curtain that separates Jimmy's side of the room from Theresa's clinks and clanks and Theresa trots out wearing her pajamas, her black, curly hair a lopsided mess.

"What's the matter?" Theresa asks.

"Natalie is missing," I say.

"Uh-oh. Where did you see her last?" Theresa peers at me.

"Home," I say.

"Let's go find her!"

"It's almost bedtime, young lady. You are not going to—" Mrs. Mattaman calls, but too late. Theresa is already flying after me.

The door bangs.

"Theresa Mattaman!" Mrs. Mattaman runs out to the balcony.

"The canteen?" Theresa calls as we pound down the stairs.

"Yeah," I call back.

Bea Trixle is just flipping the Closed sign. She picks up the cash box and turns out the lights.

"Wait—Bea?" I knock on the door.

Bea pokes her head out.

"Have you seen Natalie?" I ask.

"For goodness' sake. After all the trouble you got into yesterday, now you've lost Natalie."

Oh, how I'd like to punch Bea Trixle!

I try to keep my voice calm. "Have you seen her?"

"I most certainly have not." Bea slips out of the canteen, fits the key into the lock, and turns it.

"We better call my father," I tell Theresa.

We're just heading for the phone when Darby Trixle steps out of the dock office and beckons me with his hand. "I made a few calls. Natalie is up at the warden's house."

"The warden's house?" My voice cracks. Theresa and I look at each other. She thinks the warden is her friend?

"Yup," Darby says.

I flash back to yesterday. Natalie and Piper talking and laughing. Nat and Piper walking across the grass with books on their heads. Does Natalie think Piper is her friend?

Oh great . . . that's just what I need.

Now we're running through the sally port, which used to be some kind of Civil War something-or-other. Then we cut up to the parade-grounds level and take the back stairs through the warden's garden.

Here we are at the warden's front door again. The last place in the world I want to be. I lean over to catch my breath. Theresa hops onto the doorstep, ready to knock, when Natalie appears, scuffing her toes on the stoop.

Theresa sighs. "Thank goodness," she says.

Natalie tiptoes forward. Theresa and I fall in behind her.

What exactly am I supposed to say to Natalie? How do I explain what a snake Piper is? I mean, really . . . Natalie did everything right. She made a friend. She wrote us a note to let us know where she'd be. Isn't this what we've been telling her to do?

The moon makes a glistening, bright line on the road. Lights sparkle and shine across the bay. A boat that's anchored out dips and sways. A motorboat cuts through the water, creating a splashing white wake.

"Piper may seem like your friend, but she's not." I walk next to Natalie, which she isn't wild about, but it's too hard to talk to her if I'm walking in front or behind. Theresa skips along on her other side.

"Friend." Nat bores forward, her arms holding herself tight.

Theresa shakes her curly-haired head. "She's nobody's friend."

I kick a stone, which bumps down the road. "Theresa is right. Piper is just pretending to be your friend."

"Not pretending," Natalie mumbles, a fat gull waddling in front of her. He keeps checking back as if he knows Natalie will feed him.

"She is pretending. Some people are nice. Other people are only nice because they want something from you," I explain.

The gull hops faster, then takes off.

"Moose." Natalie drags her toe along the cement.

"What? Not *me*."

We stop by my dad's old electric shop. I peek inside. It's just the way he left it. They didn't get another electrician. If there's a problem, my dad handles it. They expect him to do everything.

"Passerini. Nice to Passerini to get on the team. Moose. Moose. Moose," she mutters.

"No, that isn't . . . Natalie, no." I start walking again.

Nat's head is cocked. Her mouth twitches.

"What's she talking about?" Theresa asks.

I groan. "She thinks I'm only being nice to this guy named Passerini because I want him to help me get on the team."

Theresa half skips down the hill. "Are you?"

I wobble my head. "That's not the only reason."

Theresa grins.

"All right, all right, maybe you have a point," I tell Natalie as we head down the 64 Building stairs, "but that doesn't mean you should trust Piper."

"Trust Piper," she mumbles.

"No, *don't* trust her. That's what I'm saying."

"Friend," Natalie says.

I sit down on the 64 Building stairs, pull off my shoe, and shake a stone out of it. Then run my hands over my hives, trying to quiet the itching. But the more I touch them, the itchier they get.

"You kinda got a problem there, Moose," Theresa whispers in my ear.

"Yeah," I sigh, "I know."

18. THE BIG STINK

▪ ▪

Monday, June 1, 1936

The next morning, the foghorns are booming. Out the front window, all you see is gray. I can't even make out the banister railing, which is five feet from the front door.

My father woke me up so I could do my garbage job before school. Now I'm going to smell like a trash can all day. Nice.

When I come into the kitchen to get breakfast, I see he has a collection of shivs. A screwdriver filed into an ice pick. A razor-sharp butter knife that could sever an artery. Bolts and razor blades fixed to a pot handle.

"Where'd you get those?"

"They start coming out of the woodwork when they hear we're going to shake down their cells. We find something like this"—he picks up the screwdriver ice pick—"they're going to the hole. We find them lying out on Broadway. No place to hide 'em when they're confined to the cells. 'Oh no, sir, never seen that before in my life,' they all say."

I swallow hard.

"Careful, Moose," he says when I pick up the really pointy one.

I don't have much time before school starts. But I may as well get started. The trash is really piling up. It's starting to stink and draw flies. No one is going to help me, either. My father is still pretty steamed.

That's okay, because I'm mad at him, too.

I imagine the look on his face if I told him the truth. Boy, would he be sorry for how he's treated me.

On the way across the balcony, I practically bump into Jimmy. The fog is that thick. It's like a wall. I can't see Berkeley or Angel Island at all.

"What are you doing up so early?" he asks.

"The warden gave me trash duty."

"That stinks, Moose."

"Funny."

He laughs; then his face gets serious. "Why is it always you?"

"What do you mean?"

He looks thoughtfully at me. "You're the guy that always ends up having to do everything."

"It's my punishment."

"For doing the right thing?"

I stare out at the gray. "Guess so."

"I'm sorry I can't help. I promised Bea I'd sweep up before school."

Jimmy goes down to the canteen. I head up to Mount Garbage.

The truck is parked by the back entrance. Overflowing trash cans are all lined up by a pile that's too big for any trash can to hold. I breathe in the smell of curdled milk, burned coffee, and pee.

I drag the first can to the edge of the truck, climb into the bed, and heave it up.

Why is it always me? It's been like this my whole life. I know I'm the healthy one. The lucky one. The strong one. But does that mean I always have to take the hit?

After the third garbage can, I develop a system. I squat down in the truck bed, work my fingers under the lip of the can, and use my leg muscles to hoist the can up. With the cans in the truck, I start on the big, raw, stinky pile.

There is rotten meat, stacks of old papers wet with spoiled milk, watermelon rinds, a box of rusted razor blades, cigarette butts, and a dead rat. Man, I wish I had gloves. This is dangerous.

After a while the stench of the pile is not so pungent, because I smell as bad as the trash.

Should I go get a broom? It's a long way down to my apartment and back up here.

I stand, surveying the great, juicy heap. Something round catches my eye. I wade deep into the mess and curve my fingers around a baseball.

A baseball? Who would throw away a perfectly good baseball?

I'm turning it in my hands when I notice the writing. At first I think it's a brand, and then I see it says *Babe Ruth*.

That couldn't be real. It has to be printed on. There's no way anyone would ever throw away a baseball signed by the Babe. I spin it in my hand. On the other side is another signature. *Al Capone*.

That one I'm familiar with. That one I know is right.

My fingers tingle as they run along the signatures.

Could it be Babe Ruth? Were his hands on this ball?

But why is it in the trash?

That's what my father was talking about this morning. The first thing they'll do when the strike is over is shake down the cells. A baseball is contraband. If a guard finds a baseball like this in a cell, the convict will be tossed into the hole.

Ordinarily the cons have more options for moving contraband around. There are spots to hide stuff in the industry buildings, the library, the barbershop, and the kitchen. But since they've been on lockdown, they don't have access to the usual hiding places.

Even so, who could throw something like this away? And how did it get in the cell house in the first place?

Who owns it now? If it's in the trash, can't I take it? Is it stealing to take trash?

"Moose?" Bo Bomini calls. I stuff the ball down my pants. It makes an enormous bulge in an incredibly embarrassing place.

"You need me to drive the truck to the incinerator?" Bomini asks. "Moose?" He frowns at me. "Everything okay?"

"Uh, sure, uh, fine." I look around. Did anyone see me take the ball? "Yeah, I need, uh, a ride."

"Hop in," he says.

I climb in, trying to figure out how to hide the bulge in my pants, which is more prominent now that I'm sitting down. I set my hands over it. But that looks weird, doesn't it?

I glance at Mr. Bomini to see if he's watching. He isn't. Phew.

Then suddenly an idea occurs to me that's so intense, I barely stifle a gasp. Can this ball get Scout and me on the team?

I don't want to let go of a baseball signed by the Babe, but getting on the team . . . that's everything.

I'll miss three weeks, but then I'll be on the team. *I'll be on the team!*

My head jerks forward each time Bomini pounces on the squeaking brake pedal.

Bomini gives me a sideways glance as we roll past the Officers' Club. "You sure look happy for a guy on trash duty."

I shrug.

"You've always had a good attitude. One of the things I like about you, Moose," Bomini says.

I cross my arms, leaning over the ball-size wedge in my pants. "Thanks, Mr. Bomini," I say.

At least he doesn't hate me.

He pulls the truck as close as he can to the incinerator and then jumps out to help me unload. I keep rearranging myself so the ball doesn't fall down my pants leg. It's pretty hard to carry garbage cans while holding a ball in your pants.

Mr. Bomini watches me. "Got a problem there, Moose?"

I turn red. "Um, no, uh," I say as the foghorn booms again. There are three of them going now. One on each end of the island and another from Angel Island.

"Climb in—I'll take you back down," Bomini says. "No offense or anything, but I hope you have time to jump in the shower before school."

"Uh-huh," I mumble. Who cares about a shower when you're holding a baseball signed by Babe Ruth. Imagine me, Moose Flanagan, with something like that.

When we get down to the dock, I realize Bomini has been talking to me and I haven't heard a word he said.

"Too bad," he says.

"Why?" I ask.

He grins. "What is up with you today?"

"Nothing," I say.

He raises his eyebrows. "I was just saying you don't need to hurry because I saw the ferry flag. No school for you."

"Why not?"

"Too foggy. I know it's going to kill you to miss school." He grins.

"It's my last day."

"Apparently they're going to have it without you."

"No, you don't understand. I have to go."

"Put on your swim trunks, then, because the ferry isn't going anywhere."

When I get to #2E, I clean off the ball, then hide it in my underwear drawer and jump in the shower. It does feel good to wash the stink off.

After the shower, my hair slicked back and a towel wrapped around my waist, I check the drawer to make sure the ball is still there.

I can't believe the ferry isn't running. That almost never happens. How am I going to get the baseball to Scout and Beck now? And whose was it, anyway? It's not like I can put up a sign in the cell house. *Will the con who dumped his contraband please see me. —Moose.*

Best thing to do is keep my mouth shut and figure out a way to get into the city.

My mother and Natalie are gone. They took an earlier boat—before the captain decided it was too foggy. I've seen it this foggy before, and the captain hasn't grounded the ferry. Just my luck.

I'm pouring myself cereal when Mrs. Mattaman and Rocky knock on the door.

This is strange. She doesn't usually knock. And why is she standing in the doorway without her apron? The only time she takes off her apron is when she goes to church.

I open the door, and she and Rocky follow me in. She hands Rocky a ball. He rolls it around her feet. She perches on the edge of the couch, her hands folded in her lap.

"You know we think the world of you, don't you?" Her dark-brown Mattaman eyes fix on me. "We couldn't love you more if you and Natalie were Mattamans."

"Yes, ma'am," I say, wondering where she's going with this.

"But things change when you get older."

"You don't think the world of me anymore?" I ask.

She grins. "Oh, Moose, you always make me laugh."

But the grin soon fades. The foghorn reverberates long and low. I can feel it in the floorboards.

Rocky sits back on his diapered bottom, takes off his shoe and sock, and waves them in the air.

"You may be thirteen—"

"Thirteen and a half," I say.

"Thirteen and a half, but you could pass for eighteen. You're taller than your father and Riv, and your face isn't babyish anymore."

I had a baby face! Lucky thing that's gone.

"People see you differently now. They expect you to act like you're eighteen."

"I'm in trouble for growing up?"

She squeezes her hands. "Did you know the warden asked Jimmy to keep an eye on Piper and he said no?" She pops up and gets Rocky, who is shaking the coffee table legs. She sits him on her lap.

"No," I say. Why didn't Jimmy tell me this?

She steadies Rocky on her knees. "I'm fond of your mother, you know I am, but she has a way of blocking out what she doesn't want to hear. Moose . . . you can't allow yourself to get into these situations."

"How could I tell the warden no?"

"Politely." She runs her fingers through Rocky's curly hair. It isn't as thick as the regular Mattaman hair yet.

"I tried, but—"

She leans forward. "Try harder."

"Okay," I say, but I'm not sure how I'm supposed to do that.

"And I do wonder what happened around that gun. Borrowing your dad's weapon, it doesn't seem like something you'd do." Her eyes drill into me.

I look away. I don't know if she found out or guessed, but she clearly doesn't believe it was me who took the gun. What about the baseball? Does she know about that too?

"You have a big heart, and you try hard to protect all of us. It's why we love you, but you mustn't throw yourself overboard."

"Yes, ma'am."

She lets Rocky down again. "Things are changing. We all need to be more watchful of Natalie. But you can't take it all on yourself. Do you understand what I'm saying?"

"Yes, ma'am," I say.

"A lot rides on what happens in the next few days." She gets up, smooths the creases in her skirt, and walks Rocky to the door holding both his hands.

"What do you mean?"

She sighs. "I can't say more than that, Moose. Just know there are a lot of people on your team. It isn't just you. We all love your father."

"Is he really up for the warden's job?"

Mrs. Mattaman twists at her hands. "You're not supposed to know that."

"He hasn't worked here that long."

"Your dad is a special person, Moose. He's moral to his core, and he's willing to stand up for what he thinks is right. We haven't had that in our leadership. It's a breath of fresh air, I'll tell you that.

"So keep your eye on Natalie, and stay away from Piper, you hear?"

"Yes, ma'am," I say, but all I'm thinking about is sneaking into the city to show Scout and Beck the baseball.

19. KEEPING MY TRAP SHUT

■ ■

Monday, June 1, 1936

I keep checking to see if the fog has lifted, but the foghorns are still booming. One side of the island, count to thirty, then the other.

They have to let the ferry go soon, don't they?

First, three weeks without baseball. Then I finally get a way onto the team, and the ferry is fogged in. The only good thing about being stuck here is that Natalie can't go to the ballpark, either. Maybe she'll forget about Passerini.

What would Babe Ruth do if he were me?

I take out his ball and roll it in my hands. Did he actually play with this ball? I imagine Babe's bat whacking it. Did he hit a home run with it? I can't wait to show Scout.

I look out the window again. The fog has got to lift soon.

If the dock officer knows I'm supposed to stay on the island, how will I sneak on the boat? I could put on my swim trunks, dip into the water, and hold on to the side. I could pretend to be unloading supplies and hide on the boat. Did my dad tell the dock officer I'm not allowed to board . . . or did he forget?

I'm trying to decide what to do when Dad bursts through the door. "Strike is over!" he announces.

"Great," I say.

"Yes." My dad sighs. "But the damage to the cell house is going to run us thousands of dollars. Then there's the money we lost on the laundry contracts, and it put us hopelessly behind in the carpentry shop. The BOP is fit to be tied."

"Oh, uh, sorry," I say.

"They're coming on Sunday for an inspection. We've got to get the place shipshape. Right now it's a shambles. Would you help out down at the dock?"

"Sure, if it will shorten my sentence. Three weeks without baseball . . . Dad, really?"

Dad takes off his hat and smooths his hair down. "Not my punishment . . ."

"Warden Williams *suggested* it. He didn't say give it to me for sure."

"Amounts to the same thing."

I groan.

My father takes off his jacket and hangs it on the hook. "I can't say I disagree with him, Moose. I don't think you understand how serious what you did was."

I don't understand? You don't understand how dangerous it is here for Natalie. You don't understand that I have to lie for her. The words spin around my mouth, but I keep my trap shut.

If I tell him the truth, he'll insist we go to the warden. And the problems the gun already caused will get bigger and more complicated.

With Natalie, it's always a judgment call she isn't capable of making, and that is so much worse.

With me, it's just a mistake.

* * *

I spend all day sweeping the dock, scrubbing algae and juicy bits of white bird poop off the decks, then the fog lifts and I unload laundry bags from the boat. I keep my book bag with me, hoping to stay on the ferry for the return run. Officer Bomini spends all afternoon by my side. It's nice of him, but inconvenient right now.

"What you got in there?" Bomini points his head toward my book bag.

"Nothing," I say.

He raises his eyebrow. "You're a man of many secrets," he says, waiting for me to get off the boat.

Now I see my other plan, swimming behind the boat, is stupid. For one thing, how would I hold on to the boat without the captain spotting me. For another, if I lost my grip, I could drown out there. I can swim, but not that far.

It's too late to play baseball anyway. I run over to call Scout. I'll tell him I can't play for a while but I have something that will get us on. But when the operator puts me through, the phone just rings and rings.

I trudge up the stairs to #2E, where Natalie is drawing pictures and Mom is sawing fat off a slab of beef.

I pour myself a glass of milk and lift the cookie jar lid, even though I know it's empty. I close it loudly so my mom will get the hint. We need cookies. But she doesn't even look over. She flips the meat, then massages spices into it. I open the bread box.

"Should have started this earlier, won't be as tender as I like. Hey, don't spoil your dinner." She points her knife at the bread.

"Surely you know by now that's impossible," I say.

She laughs.

Back in my room, I get another idea. What if Scout came to visit me . . . ? He could take the ferry over, and I could give him the ball and he could get us on the team.

I head for the living room as soon as my father comes home to see if he'll approve Scout's visit.

My mother comes running from the kitchen. He swings her in his arms. "Congratulations," she says. "I can't believe it."

She can't believe the strike is over?

"I know." He winks at her.

Then he hugs me. His hugs don't feel as good as they used to. Nobody tells you one day you'll be taller than your father, and his hugs won't be the same.

He squats down on the floor next to Natalie, who has cut out a picture of a happy bride. She's gluing it on her "happy" board.

"A little young to be getting married." He laughs.

There's something about my father that brings us together. When he's gone, Nat, my mother, and me are people who love each other. When he's home, we're a family.

He walks on tender feet to his room. I wait in the doorway until he changes out of his uniform. He blows his nose and then sticks his handkerchief in his pocket. "Did a nice job on the dock, I heard."

"Good enough to lighten my sentence?"

He sighs. "We've been through this already, Moose."

"I know. . . . I was thinking maybe Scout could come here?"

My dad shakes his head. "In the first place, I think the

warden would consider that a breach of your punishment. In the second place, there's just too much going on right now."

"We'd stay out of your way. You wouldn't even know he was here."

"I'm sorry, Moose, but you should have thought of this before you decided to waltz off with my gun."

I turn away, biting hard on my tongue. "I didn't," I mutter.

"What?" he asks.

"Nothing . . . ," I say. "Hey, are they considering you for the warden's job?"

He squints at me. "Who told you that?"

I shrug.

"You're not going to reveal your sources, huh." He smiles. "Well, I'm not at liberty to discuss that right now."

"Do you want the job?"

"Yes."

"Why?"

"More money. We're going to need it as Natalie gets older. And I think I'm up to the challenge. Which reminds me . . . do you know of any connection between Al Capone and the Esther P. Marinoff School?"

My jaw drops.

My sister applied to the Esther P. Marinoff after we moved up here, but she was turned down. Everyone was really upset. I didn't know what to do, so I wrote a note to Al Capone, asking him for help.

And then the Esther P. Marinoff changed its mind and Capone claimed credit for their reversal—but was it his doing?

"I don't know," I say. "Why are you asking *me*?"

"There were rumors Capone was involved. I don't believe it. Capone thinks FDR consults him before making any important decisions. He'll take credit for the moon if you let him. But the BOP is checking. I'm just asking because you kids"—he arches his eyebrows—"sometimes see things we don't."

He moves like his neck is sore. "Oh, I almost forgot." He digs in his pocket. Out comes an envelope with my name on it. "A little bird told me to give this to you."

I can see Piper's handwriting on the envelope. Oh great! I should toss it out without even opening it. But what if it's an apology? What if she's decided to tell the truth?

> Dear Moose,
>   I wanted to let you know that your sister and I are working together on a project that I think you'll find interesting. Very interesting.
>   I forgive you for what you did.
>   Sincerely,
>   Piper

She forgives *me*? That's rich.

I tear the letter into confetti-size pieces and throw every single one of them away.

20. TRUSTING REPTILES AND OTHER PROBLEMS

······································

Tuesday, June 2, 1936

The first thing I do as soon as I wake up is run downstairs to call Scout. But Mrs. Mattaman is using the phone, and Bea is sweeping the balcony. Whenever Bea wants to hear your phone call, she brings out her broom.

When Mrs. Mattaman finishes up, I figure Bea will go back inside. What does she care about my calls? But she doesn't. Must be a slow gossip day.

"Scout," I say when he gets on the phone, "you'll never guess what happened."

"What?" he asks.

Bea looks up.

"Something great," I say in a low voice. "I figured out a way to get us on the team for sure."

"I knew you would! Didn't I tell you you would?" He's practically shrieking. "You coming today?"

"Not today, exactly. . . . Hey, did you play with Beck and them yesterday?"

There's a long silence. The line crackles.

"Scout?"

"You weren't there. What was I supposed to do?"

"Yeah, I know. Look, I'll be there as soon as I can."

"Today?"

"No, I said not today."

"When, then? Beck just asked two other guys to join."

"He did?"

"Yep."

"I don't know when I can get there, exactly."

"Why not?"

"I got in trouble, but I'll get us on. I swear."

"You got the photo?"

"Look, just trust me. You'll never believe what I have unless you see it with your own eyes. I'll be there as soon as I can, okay?"

Back in #2E, my parents are gone. My father is at work, and my mother has taken an early boat to San Francisco to teach lessons.

The door to Nat's room is open, but she's not in there. She's not in the bathroom, or the living room, either.

Sure enough, there's a note under the saltshaker: *Gone to frnds.*

Oh great . . .

My father fixed the door so we could lock it from the inside. The key is in a blue casserole dish. Apparently Natalie knows that, or else she left when I was on the phone.

At least I know where she is.

This makes me think of Piper's letter. I'll bet she showed the letter to her father, just to make sure he knows that she's the good guy and I'm the heel and it's only out of her *great benevolence,* as our minister back in Santa Monica would say, that she forgives me.

Then I think about Scout getting to play while I'm stuck here. I'm picking up garbage and he's playing ball. I walk over to the Mattamans'. I feel lousy, and I don't want to face Piper by myself.

Mrs. Mattaman will want me to stay out of this, but I don't see how I can. Piper loves to get mixed up in my business. She works hard to make that happen. I wonder if she convinced her dad I should be the one to keep an eye on her. I wouldn't put it past her.

Theresa and Jimmy are sitting on the floor in front of the big console radio, listening to Tom Mix. Rocky is upside down, his round legs wiggling in the air. I wait for the program to end. Then I say:

"Nat's at Piper's again. Will you go up with me?"

"Sure." Jimmy hops up. Theresa is already standing by the door.

We troop up the stairs, Jimmy and I walking frontward, Theresa walking backward.

"Hey," I say. "How come you didn't tell me the warden asked you to watch Piper?"

"He didn't call me into his office or make a big deal about it the way he did with you. He asked my dad, and my mom told him to say no. She said Jimmy doesn't want to do that. You know how she is."

I laugh.

"But did you hear?" Jimmy asks. "I'm teaching Piper how to do the bookkeeping."

"Your mother must love that."

Jimmy shrugs. "Not much she can do about it. Bea's my boss."

"Did Piper say anything about what happened?" I ask as a gust of wind blows dust across the step. Theresa sneezes.

Jimmy nods. "She's upset none of us want anything to do with her."

"Yeah, and we never will, either. She got what she deserves." Theresa skips along with us, then cuts across to the parade grounds. She's back to hating Piper and won't go near her.

"What's Piper doing with Natalie?" I ask.

"Annie's gone. You, me, and Theresa stay as far from her as we can. None of the moms of the little kids will let her babysit. She needs someone," Jimmy says.

Up ahead, the lighthouse sticks up like a candle. Down by our feet a gull is hunkered, his head turned around backward and tucked into his feathers.

"But that's not the only thing going on. My dad said Capone's trying to get his man in."

"What's that supposed to mean?"

"He wants a warden who will give him special treatment, like at his other prisons."

"That's never gonna happen," I say.

"I know that, you know that, but he doesn't know that." Jimmy takes off his jacket and ties it around his waist. It's a lot warmer today than yesterday.

"I found a note from him in my dad's jacket a week or so ago. It said *Whose side are you on?*"

"Guess he's trying to figure out if he can crack your dad."

"Looking for the weak link. That's not going to be my father."

"No," Jimmy agrees.

We're at the warden's now, standing on the stoop, looking at each other. Neither one of us wants to go in.

Finally, I knock, and after a few minutes Fastball opens the door and Bug pokes her head out. "You're looking for Natalie, I take it?"

We nod.

"I'll go get her." Fastball drops his voice low, so I almost don't hear it. "Remember, you said you'd keep an eye on Bug."

"Sure, yeah, but I'm not the only one, right?" I glance at Jimmy.

Nat slides by Fastball, toe-walking out of the warden's house. She heads down the hill, and I hurry after her. "What were you doing with Piper, anyway?" I ask.

"Surprise," Natalie mumbles, flicking her chest with her chin.

"Didn't I tell you about Piper? You can't trust her."

"Trust her," Nat says.

"*Can't* trust her," I say emphatically.

Nat wraps her arms tightly around herself the way she does when she's winding up for a tantrum. I change the subject. "How'd you get the door unlocked?"

"Blue dish."

"How'd you know the key was in there?"

Nat says nothing. There's no one more effective at ignoring you than Natalie.

It's only after I get home that Fastball's words really sink in. Fastball is clearly afraid for himself, and he's afraid for Bug. I need to talk to my father about this again. How am I supposed to protect Fastball? And what about Bug? Should I have taken her right then?

21. EYES WIDE OPEN

■ ■

Tuesday, June 2, 1936

After dinner, sitting in my room, I continue stewing about Fastball and about how I'm going to get to the city. I have to secure a place on the team now. Beck said the team was full before, but clearly it wasn't. How many spaces does he have left? I have to get over there with the ball. Maybe I can sneak off the island on Sunday, when the BOP is here. We're all supposed to stay out of the way. What is more out of the way than off the island?

Everyone will be so focused on the BOP, nobody will notice me getting on the boat. Even if my father did remember to tell them to pull my card, I can easily say I have an errand to run for him in the city. I don't like to lie, but once I secure my place on the team, I can handle whatever punishment my dad doles out.

"Moose, come out here," my father calls. I lumber out in my socks.

"Dad, I wanted to talk to you about Fastball."

"I'm doing everything I can, Moose," he says.

My mother comes out of the kitchen, wiping her hands on the towel. She and my dad catch each other's eyes.

I perch on the arm of the sofa. My father sits in the chair;

my mother settles on the couch. "You'll never guess what happened today, Moose." My mother is wearing her door-to-door-salesman smile.

My eyes flash between them. Uh-oh! Something is up.

"You know how Jimmy's teaching Piper the bookkeeping for the canteen?"

"Uh-huh." I stare at her blankly.

"Well, guess who's teaching Natalie? Piper! And oh my . . . does Natalie love it. She's taken to it like a duck to water."

"She likes numbers, but—"

"Yes, she does . . . and bookkeeping is a real job. Natalie could get paid for this. Even Bea says so." My mother is so excited, she can hardly get the words out fast enough.

I stare hard at my dad. "We can't trust Piper. You know that."

Mom looks at me like I'm a clump of hair in the drain. "I know you and Piper have a lot of history," she says.

I snort.

"We know she's had a checkered past, Moose, but she and Nat have become friends." My father's voice is calm.

"Come on, Dad! You of all people should know you can't trust Piper."

He drums his fingers on the chair arm. Then fixes his eyes on me. "You don't think Piper deserves another chance?"

"No! She doesn't feel bad about what she did. She just wants to get out of trouble."

Dad sighs. "Nat isn't the easiest person in the world to connect with, and Piper is making a real effort."

I have to admit he's right about that. I've been surprised by how patient Piper has been with Natalie.

"Does Natalie have a lot of friends?" my father asks.

"Theresa."

"Theresa is ten years younger than Natalie."

"Nine, and so what?"

"Okay, nine years . . ." my mom says. "And Theresa's already started to outgrow her. Have you seen her over here recently? Piper is a lot closer to Nat's age. Besides that, Natalie doesn't learn from everyone. She and Piper have worked it out. We're not going to interfere with that."

"*Piper,* Dad?"

My dad takes a sip of coffee. "Your mother and I are working as hard as we can, but we can't save enough to support Natalie for the rest of her life. If she can get a bookkeeping job, that will really help."

"Jimmy's the one that knows bookkeeping. Why couldn't Jimmy teach Natalie?"

"Natalie and Jimmy haven't really connected. And you know you can't just switch teachers on Nat."

Once Nat gets a system down, it's set in cement, and if you alter even one tiny thing, you'll be in trouble.

"Besides that, Moose . . . Natalie has picked Piper. Shouldn't we honor that choice?"

"Not if she's going to take advantage of her."

He twirls his wedding band. "We're fully aware there are risks involved. We're going into this with our eyes wide open. But it seems like a miracle to us, and Natalie hasn't had a lot of miracles in her life. We're not going to get in the way of this, Moose. We're just not."

Miracle alert! Miracle alert! We've had more than our share of so-called miracles. There was the doctor who wanted to tie

Natalie's feet together to teach her to focus, and the clairvoy-ant who said the ghost of our great-grandfather was trying to get our attention through Natalie's tantrums. There were the doctors who wanted to study her brain after she died, and there was the minister who believed her only problem was an incomplete religious education. We've had a million miracles that didn't amount to a pile of dog crap. The only things that have really helped Natalie are Carrie Kelly and the Esther P. Marinoff.

Not Piper . . . what is the matter with them?

22. THE BUTTON RING

■ ■

Sunday, June 7, 1936

On Sunday morning, I put on my baseball clothes and get my gear together. I called Scout last night and told him I'd be there today. The game won't start until after church, but I want to be ready.

My mom sends me to the canteen for milk, and Bea marks down the cost on our chart. Then she looks up. "Congratulations," she says. "Have they set a date?"

"A date? For what?"

"Natalie's wedding. She's been cutting out wedding dresses from the Sears Roebuck catalog. She's been talking my ear off about veils, shoes, jewelry—"

I stop, the milk bottle cold in my hand. "Talking your ear off? Natalie?"

"Okay." Bea seesaws her head. "Maybe it's me been doing more of the talking. But she is excited. Oh my, she is."

"Come on, Bea. You know Natalie isn't getting married."

Bea slips her glasses on her head. "She showed me her ring."

"What ring?"

"It was a bit unusual, but you know how she loves those buttons."

"I don't know what you're talking about," I mutter. I stare out the window. The sky is full of soft, puffy clouds. The *Coxe* is pulling in. I'm going to take the eleven a.m. Everyone will be absorbed in last-minute preparations. Nobody is going to care.

"I got married when I was seventeen. And so did Anna Maria Mattaman," Bea natters on.

I squint at her. "Who is she supposedly marrying?"

"That Passerini fella, of course. Where have you been, Moose? That's all she talks about."

"She's not marrying Passerini." I bite the inside of my cheek, walking as fast as I can away from Bea's trouble-making mouth.

"Tell Natalie that," Bea calls after me.

We'll all be dead and still Bea will be talking. I try to push her words out of my mind, but I can't.

In our apartment, Natalie is sitting on the floor by the book-shelf. I glance at her hand. The button Passerini gave her is tied to her finger with thread. Is that what Bea was talking about?

"That's not a wedding ring, Nat," I inform her.

"Wedding ring," she mutters, sticking her hand out.

"It's not. You're not getting married. He was just being nice."

"A nice man to marry you," Nat mutters.

That's what Dad always says. I could kill him right now. "He is nice, but he's too young to get married, and he's not even your boyfriend."

"Husband," Nat says.

"Mom!" I run into the kitchen. "Did you hear that? She thinks Passerini is going to marry her. Will you talk to her?"

"Oh honey, don't be silly. It's just girl talk. I did the same thing when I was her age."

"Mom, she's telling everyone she's getting married. You know how literal she is."

"Nobody believes her."

"Bea does."

My mother flaps her dish towel at me. "Well, you know what her opinion is worth."

"He's a sophomore, Mom."

"Is he concerned about this?" She picks up a plate and begins to dry it. "Has he talked to you?"

"I don't know what he thinks. I've been stuck here."

"Well then . . . no sense in borrowing trouble."

"But I'll see him in two weeks!"

"Look"—she fixes her eyes on me—"I will make sure she doesn't embarrass you, all right?"

"That's not fair, and it's not what I said."

"You're the healthy one, Moose. And with that health comes responsibility."

My insides begin to boil. I would really like to put my fist through the wall right now. "Mom, I know!"

"All right then. End of discussion."

"Where is she going to be during the BOP visit?" I ask.

"She'll be with me, and then if there's time, your father will introduce her to the men from the BOP. He wants to address any objections up front."

"Where will she be *until then*?" I huff.

"Until when?"

"Until Dad introduces her."

"I just told you, Moose . . . with me."

All the air shoots out of me. "Just make sure she doesn't go near Piper, okay?"

"All right, you've made your point." Her voice is strained. Her jaw has gone hard.

"I'm just trying to keep her safe."

Mom wheels around. "You don't want her around Passerini. You don't want her around Piper. Where do you want her?"

"Mom, stop it! Look . . . you've always said not to trust Piper. Not to go near her, and now . . ."

Her shoulders soften. "I know I did. But Piper is on to something here. If Nat can learn a trade, if she can learn bookkeeping, she can hold a job. A year ago I would never have believed that was possible."

"Piper's only doing this because she's getting something out of it."

"Okay, fine, but Natalie is the one getting the most out of it. Once she has a skill, the world will open up for her."

I reach down to the hot hive on my ankle and scratch it so hard it bleeds.

It's sweltering in our apartment. I head down to the dock, hoping for a breeze by the water.

The sun beats down on my head, making my hair feel like a burning wig. I climb down the rocks. It's peaceful—just the gentle slapping of the bay against the dock struts. I splash my face, and peel off my shoes and socks and stick my feet in the water.

A lot of guys don't like to play ball when it's this hot. But I don't mind.

I try to think about ways to improve my game, but my mind returns to Piper the way your tongue finds food between your teeth.

Maybe she's being nice to Natalie to earn points with her dad. It stinks to have people distrust you, but she shouldn't use Natalie that way.

The sweat slides down my sides. My shirt is stuck to my back as I watch people get off the ferry. A group of religious men comes across the gangplank. I wonder why there are so many of them. They're here because of the BOP, I guess. Prisoners look more respectable when they're seated in church services.

The BOP visit has been planned down to the letter: a tour of the cell house, the cons' baseball game, and then apple pie.

I'm going to run up to our sweatbox of an apartment, get my gear, and just walk onto the boat.

On the balcony, I hear the truck horn *toot-toot*. Bea is taking a load of groceries up the hill—lumpy sacks of potatoes—as well as stainless-steel pots big enough to feed an army. But who is that with her?

Natalie and Piper.

Wait . . . where is my mother?

23. BASEBALL, BEA, AND THE BOP

■ ■

Sunday, June 7, 1936

I shouldn't worry about this.

It's not my business.

Still, there's a lot of time before the ferry leaves. I may as well confirm Nat's at the Officers' Club. I don't want to be worrying about her when I'm playing ball. I can't let anything get in the way of my game.

I hurry up the back stairs of 64 Building, which are socked in with hot, still air, and then cut across to the switchback. Ahead is the Officers' Club, where the wives and kids are beginning to congregate.

Inside, people are in their church clothes. The chairs are set up for the service. Theresa, Jimmy, and Rocky are playing sardines with a gaggle of little boys.

My mother is sitting at the piano, playing a hymn. "Mom." I rush over to her. "Where is Natalie?"

Mom ignores me until she's done.

"What, Moose?" she asks.

"Where's Natalie?"

"She went with Piper. Bea needed help."

"Mom!"

"Calm down, she'll be right back." My mom turns the pages of her music and starts on a new hymn.

I go outside, drifting up the hill by the morgue. Bea must have wanted Piper and Natalie to help her unload. Bea won't lift anything heavier than a can of soup. I'll go up and walk Natalie back down to the church service, and then I'll get on the ferry. I'll have to sneak out in the middle of the service, but I can manage that.

At the water tower, Officer Harrison trots toward me, shaking his head. He taps his clipboard then holds two fingers in the air. "Two places you can be right now. Your apartment or the Officers' Club. That is it."

"Yes, sir."

I make a show of walking back down to the club. Once I'm out of Officer Harrison's line of sight, I cut back around and take the stairs to the warden's back garden.

It's quiet up top. The road has been swept. The warden's stoop sparkles like a giant tongue has licked it clean. Bright-red flowers bloom from the planters by the door. The trash was burned this morning; I can still smell the smoke of the incinerator. The trash cans have been scrubbed shiny inside and out.

Up ahead I see Officer Trixle, his uniform newly starched and ironed. I duck behind the warden's house.

The ferry whistles.

I'm steamed at my mom. She said she'd keep her eye on Natalie. I could take a later ferry, but then I'm afraid I'll run into my father with the BOP men waiting at the dock in Fort Mason.

I'm hurrying to the back entrance of the cell house when I see Piper running hard like she's scared.

"Where's Natalie?" I ask.

"The cell house," she gasps. "I was just looking for you."

"WHAT?"

Piper leans over, holding her sides. "Bea told her to take a physical inventory of the supplies in the cell house."

"Come on, Piper. That's crazy. You're making this up."

She shakes her head. "No."

The sweat drips down my nose and into my mouth.

"She's inside the cell house," Piper huffs.

"That's impossible. How would she get in?"

"I don't exactly know."

"Then how can you be sure she's in there?"

"Bea sent me down to get coffee cups from the Officers' Club. When I came back, I think I saw Natalie curled inside one of those giant soup pots."

"You *think*?"

"I'm pretty sure. The kitchen cons were already carrying the pots. I asked Bea. She said no, but she was lying, Moose."

"She was lying, or you're lying or mistaken," I say. But something bothers me about this. If Nat was upset, she would definitely crawl inside a giant pot. She feels safe in small spaces.

"Let's assume you're right."

"I am right, I swear to God."

"Why would Bea do that?"

"If they find Natalie in the cell house, your dad will be

out of the running. And the next guy in line after my father and your father is Darby. Bea wants Darby to be the warden, or at least assistant. Remember how mad they got when your father was promoted?"

"Why didn't you stop her?"

"It was too late."

"Don't lie to me."

"I'm not!" Piper shouts.

My mind is spinning. I'm having trouble breathing.

Do I tell my mother? Or Mrs. Mattaman? Run into the Officers' Club in the middle of church services? What about my father? Is there any way to get ahold of him? Should I find Officer Bomini?

But all these things will take too long. If Nat's in the cell house, every second counts.

My legs fly down the hill. The soles of my shoes slap the cement.

Get her out. Get her out. Get her out. I suck in each stinging breath.

My father's guard's uniform. It's a little small for me, but . . . I look like the Nose. Everybody says so. I can pass for him.

Officer Trixle motions me to stop as I pound down the hill.

Spit flies from my mouth, spraying my nose. "Going home!"

I cut back behind 64 and clatter down the stairs.

The apartment door bangs behind me.

I rip off my trousers and slide my legs into my father's

pants and my sticky, wet arms into his shirtsleeves. My feet jam into his too-small shoes. My toes curl up, crammed in the toe. I grab his jacket and run.

I'm flying toward the door, when it hits me.

This is a trap. Piper doesn't want my father to be the warden, because then her father won't be. She'll deny telling me Natalie is in the cell house. Nobody heard Piper say it except me. Mrs. Mattaman warned me about this.

But if it is true, what will happen to Natalie? I can't take the chance.

I thunder across the balcony. The jacket flies back. I try to button it and hold the cap as I run.

But wait. . . . A guard wouldn't run unless it was an emergency. This is an emergency, but I can't show it.

In the stairwell, where no one can see, I pull myself up the steps three at a time. At the top I consider my options.

Am I in a guard tower's line of sight? What about Darby Trixle? But I look like a guard, so it should be okay.

The back stairway. It's faster. I tear up the stairs.

I'll come out at the top of the switchback and walk into the cell house, as if I were him.

What if the Nose is already in the cell house?

That's a chance I have to take.

The sweat pours down my chest. The scratchy shirt is soaked through. I pull the cap low and approach the front of the cell house, the flag rippling behind me. I walk up the steps, my pulse throbbing. My hand slips on the handle. I grip it harder and swing it open.

The glaring lights of the control room, the hub of the prison, are before me. I blink.

My head feels thick. My heart pounds. Someone will stop me. But the control room officer has his head down, studying a clipboard. He twinkles his fingers to motion me in.

24. THE IRON MAIDEN

■■■■■■■■■■■■■■■■■■■■■■■■■■■■■■■

Sunday, June 7, 1936

The second sally port door clatters open, and I walk through. The door closes behind me, and I stand there, caught in the iron maiden. Doors locked in front. Doors locked behind. The thick metal radiates a sweltering heat. The floor moves up toward me like a swelling wave. *Clank*—the door in front opens, and I walk forward.

Slowly the insanity of what I'm doing sinks in. I've never been on the inside. I don't know how the place is laid out. I can't ask for directions. The Nose would know his way around.

I try to push the terrible thoughts about what could be happening to Natalie out of my head.

"You're early. Just couldn't stay away from us, eh?" The officer comes out of the control room, but his eyes are on the next barred metal door. He sticks his key in and unlocks it.

I answer him with a nod, afraid to open my mouth or meet his eyes. I look like the Nose, but I don't sound like him.

How does the Nose walk? How does he carry himself? What are his cell-house duties? I stick my hands in my pockets and try to steady myself.

Kids aren't allowed here, or women, either. Certainly not girls.

A girl in the cell house!

A regular girl would know the dangers, but Natalie …
My stomach dips.

The cell house is full of "abominably wicked men." Mr.
Mattaman told me that once.

I try to calm my queasy stomach. Try to think this
through. What do I know?

The shape of the cell house is a long rectangle the size of
an airplane hangar. I was in the hospital here once. Where
was that?

"Erickson!" somebody yells. "Come look at this." It takes
me a few beats to realize that Erickson is the Nose's name.

I pull my cap lower and head toward the officer with the
big red ears—I forget his name—into a room three times the
size of a gymnasium, with cells—cages—stacked three high.
My mouth drops open.

I snap it closed. The Nose has seen this lots of times. He
wouldn't look around like a wide-eyed kid. I walk forward
down the aisle marked *B-1*. B-1? Is that Broadway?

Both sides of the aisle have jail cells stacked upon jail
cells. Each has a cot, a sink, a toilet, and a small shelf attached to the wall. Some are empty. Some have a man inside.
One prisoner stands holding the bars, another lies facedown
on his narrow cot, a third waves to me from his toilet.

Across the way a man has his head bent over a stack of
thick books. A humpbacked guy brushes his teeth. Another
stares with hard, angry eyes. I keep walking down the path-
way of light.

"Hey, Erickson, my man," a prisoner shouts down from
an upper cell. "Got two packs on Flanagan."

Two packs? Cigarettes. They trade them like money. Are they betting who will be the next warden?

The sounds of my footsteps reverberate in the cavernous building. I'm careful to keep my distance from the red-eared officer.

In the cell I see a convict named Lizard. He has a towel over his head, held in place with his cap. His sheet is wrapped around him like a dress. His bed is bare, just a mattress with striped ticking. He's walking back and forth in his cell chanting, "Here comes the bride. All dressed in white."

I shudder. This couldn't be about Natalie, could it?

Lizard's eyes shift like a reptile's. Does he recognize me? I hold my breath, waiting for him to call me out. But he says nothing.

Red Ears bangs his clipboard against the bars of Lizard's cell. "Cut it out, Lizard, or I'll slap you in the hole."

Lizard rearranges his pillowcase veil. "Ain't going to do that today, are you, sir. Got to be clean as a whistle in there."

"I wouldn't test that particular hypothesis," Red Ears says, and then turns to me. "In early to get in good with the boss, are you, Erickson? Well, we can use the extra help."

I swallow hard. "Uh-huh," I mumble.

Red Ears seems to take this in stride. My mumble hasn't given me away, but I don't dare say more.

I try to walk like I know where I'm going. The soup pots must be in the kitchen. But where is that? I walk straight ahead, praying this is the way.

"You tell the warden it ain't my fault," a con doing one-handed push-ups shouts between breathy counts.

Each cell is a large dog's cage. How evil must you be to get put in a cage?

I keep walking until I see the dining room and, behind that, the kitchen! Please let Natalie be okay. Please please please. I pick up the pace now that I know I'm going in the right direction.

In the empty dining hall, I see a short guy with an egg-shaped head cleaning the steam table.

Fastball! In a white shirt, white pants, and a cook's hat. The kitchen con uniform.

Why is he here and not in the warden's house? Oh yeah, Dad said the BOP doesn't like the cons working as pass men.

Fastball does a double take. "She's here," he hisses. "Go get her a con uniform. Down one floor. We can't hide her in a dress."

"She's okay?" My voice breaks. My collar is so tight, it's choking me.

"Yes." He looks me up and down. "Get two. There can't be two Noses."

Should I find Natalie first? Or trust a criminal?

25. A GIRL IN THE CELL HOUSE

▪ ▪

Sunday, June 7, 1936

I grab the banister to steady myself and then take the steps down to the long line of shower nozzles, empty but dripping, like a naked murderer was just there. My heart slips sideways.

My mind flashes on the shivs my father showed me.

It's steamy and hot down here. I creep into the clothing-issue room. The sight of the orderly white bins with the folded blue shirts and the long rows of shoes and shaving brushes calms me.

I've seen my father take a con out of the cell house to help paint or rewire 64 Building. Nat will put on a convict's uniform, and then I'll walk her out of here.

In the back corner, an officer with a large, squarish head consults his clipboard. At the wire mesh wall, an old convict with no chin—just a slide of freshly shaved flesh—looks at me, his uneven eyes shifting uncertainly. I remember my father said the clothing-issue guy knows the name, size, and number of every con in the cell house.

"Officer Erikson." He swallows. The square-headed officer looks up.

"I'll take two," I tell the convict.

The con's eyes dart back to Officer Square Head.

Square Head stands up from his desk. "What's this about, Erickson? No new men today, you know that."

Hives have sprouted on my legs, hot and unbearably itchy. I lean down to scratch them. "Going to show the BOP how the system works," I mumble.

"Have to have the proper paperwork—"

"Assistant Warden Flanagan's orders." I try to sound sure of myself.

The convict looks to Square Head. He chews at his lip and then shrugs. "Give him 571 and 572. We'll check 'em back in tonight."

The convict pulls two pairs of shoes and socks, shirts and slacks, and sets them in two neat piles on the counter.

Square Head walks toward me, looking down at my too-short pants. "Laundry deliver the wrong trousers, Erickson?"

My stomach cramps. "Uh-huh," I mumble, glancing at my socks, which are all too visible.

He laughs and shakes his head. "Seen one guard come in with three legs on his pants. They're rough on the new guys."

I try to smile, like a good sport, but I'm busy wondering, How would the Nose hold this stuff? Not close against his chest like a little old lady. I rejigger the bundles and manage to get the clothing up the stairs without dropping anything. Another officer is walking high above, in the gun gallery. His footsteps make the metal structure shake. I take a wobbly breath and transfer the bundles to one arm and wave with the other.

"Thought you were in later?" he shouts down.

I shrug, then walk away, as if I had pressing business elsewhere. Then I scoot around the long steam table at the back of the dining hall and enter the sweltering kitchen holding my breath. I walk by the glass booth with the mess officer inside. *Don't look up. Don't look up.*

He looks up, but his eyes are glazed, as if he's thinking hard about something else. I keep walking.

Fastball is mixing apple slices in a bowl. He angles his head toward a room at the back of the kitchen.

I scurry by him, my heart beating loudly.

She's there!

Her hair is wet with sweat, and she's kneeling down, counting jars of jelly. In Bea's green dress, she looks as out of place as a domino in a checkers set.

I kneel down next to her. "Are you okay?"

She digs at her chest with her chin.

I pull the clothes out of the bag. "It's going to be hard to get out of here. Could you put these on?"

Her mouth moves from one side to the other like it's an elastic band stretching in all directions. She doesn't take the clothes.

"Please," I beg. "For me."

She bites at her hand. "Hey, Pass, Passerini, Passerini."

Oh no. Not here. She can't lose control here. "Natalie, listen . . . please, do what I say—"

A weird, hot breeze makes the tiny hairs on my neck stand up, and then I see something move. A man . . . there's a man behind the flour bag!

"Get out," I shout as he rises up. He's huge, twice my weight. A wall of steel with pumped shoulders and tattooed arms.

"She's mine."

"Passerini. Pass. Passerini. No, no, no!" Natalie whipsaws her hair.

I leap toward him. "Get away!" I squeeze the words through my swollen throat. Then I see the metal blade in his hand.

"NOT MY SISTER." I grab the flour scooper and go after him like I'm the one with the serious weapon. There's a rushing in my ears.

I grab him by his thick neck and do my best to dig the flour scooper into his massive shoulder.

He flings me off like a fly. His knife scrapes my arm.

I jump up and punch him hard in his bricklike gut.

He grabs me, ready to sink the shiv in my neck, but I kick him so hard, the knife goes flying across the room.

"Ow!" he cries.

He doubles back to Natalie. "Ain't you a pretty one."

She kicks him hard in the shin, startling him. "Passerini!" she shouts, and then Fastball appears.

"Fang! Get out of here!"

Fang scowls. "That's right, you're a rat now."

"Out!" Fastball glares at him.

Fang smiles an oily smile. "That kitten goin' to have his last meow." He mimes squeezing Bug's neck and tearing her head off, and then slips out of the room.

Fastball's face turns the color of old undershirts. "Hurry," he tells me.

"Nat—" I gasp for breath, leaning against the shelves, wiping my bleeding arm on my pants leg. "We have to get out of here."

Her eyes move left to right across the floor. "Passerini," she says.

"I know. Passerini. Put these clothes on."

"Passerini, marry him." She rocks onto her toes.

Sweat drips off my chin. "Sure, of course, you'll marry him. Just put these on, Nat, please!"

Fat Fogarty is behind Fastball. I don't like the way he's looking at Natalie, either. I close the pantry door, blocking his view of her.

When I open the door again, Natalie has changed. But even in convict clothes, she still looks like a girl.

It's the hair.

Fastball sees it, too. "Here." He hands her his white baker's cap. "Put this on."

Natalie slips it on. She looks more like a boy now, but the baker's cap is out of place with a regular convict's uniform.

"Erickson, what are you doing?" The officer in the kitchen leans his head outside the glass booth.

"Don't say anything," I whisper to Natalie, my heart banging my chest.

"Got a little problem in Sixty-Four," I say.

"What kind of a problem?"

My mind spins. "Bea Trixle got a shipment she can't move."

As soon as I say this, I know it's a mistake. This isn't a dire enough situation for them to allow a con out on BOP day.

"Not today, and don't let Bea Trixle tell you otherwise."

"Yes, sir." I turn Nat around and push her back.

I can feel him looking at me. "Who is that, anyway?"

The sweat drips off my face. "Five Seventy-One," I say.

"Five Seventy-One? Must be new. Fish aren't allowed out. You should know that."

"Yes, sir," I say.

I walk back to the pantry with Nat.

Fastball breezes by me. "The Nose is here," he says, and I dive back into the little room with Natalie, rip off the guard jacket, and pull on the convict shirt, though this seems like the world's worst idea. How will I get out of here as a convict? That really is impossible. But there can't be two Noses.

I go out into the kitchen to ask for Fastball's help. Immediately, I hear the news fly from con to con: "B-O-P. B-O-P. B-O-P. B-O-P."

I push Nat back into the pantry. "Count something."

"Already counted."

I look around. "Tear up bread for the birds."

"On-duty officers eat here, too," my father's tour-the-cell-house voice booms.

I close the pantry door.

"Doors open," the kitchen officer barks.

I open the door, grab a broom, and busy myself sweeping in the doorway, careful to block Natalie. My hands tremble as I work the broom under the lip of the shelves.

"We make a thousand meals a day in this room. Food's pretty good. Can't beat the franks and beans," my father tells the three men in black suits.

The bald BOP guy fans his face with the program. "Always this hot in here?"

My father flashes by, surveying the spanking-clean

countertops, floors, pots, and knives on the silhouette board. He doesn't see me.

"Up these stairs to the hospital." His voice recedes.

I wait until I can't hear him anymore. My arms are trembling. I'm just getting Nat gathered up when the count bell rings.

Oh great.

An officer knows his men. They've all been distracted by the BOP, but it will be obvious when the count comes up plus two.

The kitchen crew shuffles into the cafeteria. The officer barks at them, and the men count off. I duck back into the dark pantry with Natalie, but Natalie gravitates toward the sound of numbers.

I grab her arm.

She shakes me off. Her hands flap like she's touched a hot stove. This is too much for her—she's slipping away.

26. YOU CAN'T OPEN A WINDOW IN PRISON

■ ■

Sunday, June 7, 1936

I jump in front, blocking her. She stops, her face twitching.

I listen until the count is done and the men have marched out.

The dining hall is empty, but we can't hide here for long. They'll be back for pie. Where can we go?

The chapel. They must be done with the chapel by now. But where is it?

The library. I can keep Natalie hidden behind the stacks, memorizing the indexes of books. I don't know where that is, either.

I can't just go wherever I want. Convicts aren't allowed to walk freely about the cell house.

I think there may be some kind of butcher shop under the kitchen. The thought of convicts with knives makes my legs wobble.

But a butcher wouldn't be in there now, right? Not everyone goes to the rec yard. The men in the hospital, the men in the hole, the new fish, anyone with a mark against him during the workweek, will be on lockdown in the cell house. But no one is at work during the rec yard time. At least, I don't think so.

We'll slip down the stairs and turn in the other direction. We'll hide until the BOP leaves, and then I'll jump into my father's officer uniform again and get Natalie out.

We sneak down the stairs. I sneak, anyway. Natalie walks. Her eyes on her feet.

The clothing exchange and the showers are empty. I turn toward the butcher shop.

Nobody is down there right now. Every man is counted every half hour. They always know where everyone is. But the guards are human . . . they make mistakes.

My hands shake as we walk down the hall under the kitchen. I see a small room set up like a church. Chairs face the pulpit. A small wooden altar with Jesus on the cross stares down at us.

Of course, there are lots of religious men here today. They couldn't all give services at the chapel. They must have set up other rooms. But then I see that there are men inside: a big priest and a convict sit with their backs to us, their heads bent over open Bibles.

I stand stock-still, stupid as a roast beef.

It's so hot down here, it's hard to think.

Of course it's hot. You can't open the windows in prison.

Natalie holds one arm with the other and rocks. Her eye has begun to twitch. She's losing her grip.

The big priest has taken his robe off. It's on a hanger, hooked on a coatrack.

The robe is a dress. Kind of. With a hood.

Nat could put it on. She could walk right out of the cell house in it.

All I have to do is duck in there and slip the robe off the

hanger. But how? The door will squeak, the handle will click, the priest will hear. I can't even risk rattling the handle to test if it's locked.

Natalie is rocking more wildly, nicking her chest with her chin.

I tiptoe to the door and check the handle, moving it barely a sixteenth of an inch to see if the lock breaks the motion. It does not. I exert more pressure until the mechanism releases its grip on the door with a dull click.

I freeze. The blood empties out of my head.

But the two men are bent over their Bibles. They don't look up. I hold the door cracked open an inch, but it's so quiet. There's no way I can go in and not be heard.

I've just decided to give up and return the door, increment by increment, to the jamb, when music . . . I hear music. The priest and the prisoner are singing. They walk toward the altar, their voices in harmony, their backs to me.

I push open the door, my ears keen for a sound that could give me away. I take a big breath, dart in, and snatch the robe. The heavy cloth weighs down my arm.

The hanger swings empty. I slip out the door before it closes again.

My whole body shakes as I catch the door, then as quietly as possible click it back in place.

I let out my breath, wind the robe around my arm, and turn toward Natalie. But Natalie is not there.

27. IN THE SHADOW OF THE WALL

■ ■

Sunday, June 7, 1936

I try to breathe. She was just here.

A cell door slams above me. I jump.

Did she run away, or was she taken?

I don't care that I'll get in trouble. I don't care about my father's job. I don't care about anything except please, God, let Natalie be safe.

I move as quietly as possible back to the showers. The big green room is empty. Just the drip of one nozzle. *Drip, drip, drip.*

A line of men walks up the stairs. I duck around the corner and hold my breath, watching each man's legs disappear up the stairwell. Nat's pants are too long. They hang over her shoes. But every pair of pants legs on these stairs is the exact right length.

I run back past the temporary chapel to the dark butcher shop.

I smell meat and sharp bleach. A big icebox is in the back. She wouldn't hide in there, would she?

My heart beats in my ears. I run to the icebox and yank it open. A pig's head with glassy, half-closed eyes looks out at me.

I clamp my hand over my mouth, stifling a scream. Then I turn and dash out of the butcher shop and back upstairs.

Above me, the sound of marching feet. I scoot back into the stairwell. A line of convicts walks in lockstep toward the rec yard door.

I wait. Watching. Hoping.

She's there!

I stuff the robe down the front of my shirt and run after them. The thick roll of fabric presses against my belly. I rearrange it until it looks like I have a good-size gut and fall in behind her. My legs have gone wobbly, but the marching helps.

"Nat," I whisper.

The line of men stops. Nat barely keeps from running into the man in front of her. Officer Adams calls up to the gun-gallery guard, who lowers the key on a pulley. He walks the big key over to the rec yard door and slips it into the lock.

My father's voice wafts through my head. *The prison yard is a little piece of hell. Things happen there you don't ever want to know about.*

Officer Adams steps back and waits for the crew to file through.

He'll notice two strange people. Of course he will.

We're almost there. I brace myself for his response.

"Adams, you poor sap." The Nose comes around the corner and waggles his eyebrows at Adams.

Officer Adams turns away as we pass through. "I got my money on Williams. You?"

"I'm a Flanagan man," the Nose tells him.

The rec yard door opens on to a narrow stairway, which leads down to a football field of concrete with cement terraces cut into one side. The guards in the small mesh tower rooms have their rifles trained on us. A fifteen-, sixteen-, maybe twenty-foot wall pens us in, casting a long shadow across the yard.

With the robe on, Natalie can walk back into the building. But do priests go out into the yard? And how do I get her to put the robe on without everyone seeing?

If she has a tantrum here, will they shoot her?

I stick to Nat like butter to bread. Down the stairs we go, and over to the south corner, where the bridge players sit on makeshift stools.

Across the yard, the handball players line up. In the east corner, a guy is setting the base bags for baseball. Clusters of men sit on the cement terraces, watching the ships.

Then I see the rabbi. He's talking to a man who is banging his foot against the fence.

They do come out here!

My eyes settle on the bridge players. Could she duck behind them? Could Fastball get a group together? A crowd of convicts surrounding Natalie?

I gag.

No.

I stick with Nat as she dips her hand into her pocket and begins to feed the birds.

Oh no, not here. But wait . . . the birds. Could they help?

At first the crumbs collect at her feet. And then a fat gull flies down, and more swoop in.

Flat yellow feet, gray-and-white feathers. Sharp beaks. Shrill cries.

The cement is covered with birds.

"What's going on?" a guard with a megaphone shouts down from the mesh guard cage.

The Nose waves his arms, shooing birds. A few scatter, but they don't go far. New birds swoop down. The cons gather around.

Nat has to finish her breadcrumb ritual. She can't stop midway.

More birds fly overhead.

Nat's pockets are flat. The bread is almost gone. The flapping wings die down.

Now!

"Natalie," I say. "I have a dress for you. Put it on and you can go home."

She squints. Her face screws up. Her routine, feeding the birds, has revived her. She's trying again.

"Girls wear dresses," I tell her. "Passerini said so."

I pull the robe out of my pants, searching for the head opening. When I find it, I stick my hand through, lift it over her head, and pull up the hood.

Nat shudders, her arms stiff at her sides. I don't think she likes the hood, but she doesn't yank it off.

"Home," I say in a low voice.

The birds scatter across the pavement.

Nat grimaces. Her eyes move wildly, left to right.

"Home," she mumbles, her arms tight against her sides. The Nose stands by me now. His dark eyes watch us.

He knows.

Nat tastes her lip with her tongue and walks stiff-legged, her priestly robe belt hanging loose around her middle.

The Nose turns to me. "I'll make sure she gets out," he whispers.

"What the heck was that about?" Officer Adams comes trotting up.

Fat Fogarty steps in. "You know how them birds are."

"I know how they are when somebody feeds them," Officer Adams barks.

"I told you somebody been stealing bread." Fastball is on one side of Officer Adams. Fat Fogarty is on the other.

"Always got an answer, don't you, Fastball? If I were the warden, I sure wouldn't have you in my house," Adams says.

"I'm aware of that, sir."

Officer Adams points his chin to the cell-house door. "Scared that poor priest out of his wits. You know how hard it is to get a good religious man out here?"

We watch Natalie disappear into the big house.

"You got any more tricks up your sleeve?" Adams walks up close to Fastball.

"It wasn't me, sir," Fastball says.

Adams rolls his eyes. "Of course not. It's never you, is it? Well, get the word out, because I've got all those brand-spanking-clean seg cells, if you catch my drift."

"I do, sir. I catch your drift."

"You're up for probation, aren't you?"

"Yes, sir." Fastball nods.

"Wouldn't want to risk that, would you?"

"No, sir."

"I suppose it don't matter much. You get out and you'll

be right back in; place is sticky as glue, isn't that right, Fast-ball?"

Fastball turns white as a scar. "No, sir," he says. "I'm not coming back."

"Well, we'll see, won't we?" He smiles his fat smile at Fastball. Fastball doesn't smile back.

28. THE CURVEBALL

■ ■

Sunday, June 7, 1936

The shade is crowded out here. I'd rather stay in the beating-down hot sun than stand in the middle of a pack of murderers.

I find Fastball pulling baseball bats out of a burlap bag. Fang is a few feet away. A chill goes up my spine. "Meow," Fang says. Fastball's hands tremble.

"I need to get out of here," I tell Fastball.

"Welcome to the club," he mumbles. "You gonna play?"

I watch a man built like a concrete mixer take a spin around the periphery of the yard. Got to be safer playing ball, doesn't it? "Sure," I say.

I'm just walking to the dugout when I see Al Capone.

He's stocky, with thick legs and arms. He's got black hair, broad eyebrows, thick lips, a square face, and a scar down one side—the ghost of a line from his ear to his lip. He moves like an armored vehicle.

He's walking toward me slowly, deliberately.

In Atlanta they said he operated his mob from behind bars, but he's alone. He doesn't have a gang here . . . does he?

Fastball slants his head toward Capone. Under his breath he says: "They trot him out for the BOP. They all want to go home and say they shook hands with the big fellow."

Capone has a slow, unnerving smile. He drills into me with those piercing eyes. "Why, if it isn't Moose Flanagan. Heard you got something of mine."

The pavement burns through the thin soles of my convict shoes. I swallow hard. "Sir?"

"You heard me."

"How'd you get it in here?" I ask.

He tosses a baseball from one beefy paw to the other. "You think I'm gonna go running my mouth to the warden's son?"

"I'm not the warden's son."

"Not yet."

"I—"

"The Babe's signature . . . and mine. Not another one like that. What you going to do with it?"

Should I say I'm going to give the ball back to him?

My knees wobble underneath me. "Well, uhh, there's, uh, my high school team. And I really want to get on it."

He snorts. "You gonna hand my ball over to some punk to get on your own school team? Smarten up, kid."

I swallow hard. "The captain, Beck, he's—"

"Yeah, yeah, I see. You gonna be his little girl. That what you want?"

"No, sir, that's not—"

"What?" he roars.

"No, sir!" I shout.

"Stand your ground or I want that ball back."

"Yes, sir."

"What?"

"Yes, sir!" I shout.

"Glad we got that squared away. Now, you playing with me?"

Fastball steps forward. "He's with us."

"Had enough of me, is that right, Fastball? Even after all I done for you." Capone laughs.

"You lost me when you went to bat for Trixle," Fastball says. "You hate him."

Capone shrugs. "The man's useful. His wife likes the finer things. Flanagan don't play the game."

Fastball shakes his head.

"That's the way it works. Better learn that before you walk out of here."

"Not going to play it that way."

Capone shrugs. He heads for the pitcher's plate. "Suit yourself."

Pitcher? I heard Capone played first base, like me.

I watch him warm up. He weaves his fingers together and thrusts his hands over his head. He does knee bends and cracks his thick bull neck. Then he pitches some warm-ups to the catcher.

"Let's play ball," he calls, and I step up to bat.

Adrenaline rushes through me. My hands twitch as they hold the bat.

He pitches a soft one. A little high. I hold myself in. I know a ball when I see one.

"Strike," he calls.

Strike? That wasn't a strike. I bring the bat down, about to say something. But this is Al Capone. I hold my tongue.

Next one comes slow and easy—a juicy meatball.

I'm going to smack the soft heart of it. That ball is going

to fly out of everyone's reach. I can sense it in my fingers, but at the last minute I hold back. It flies south of the strike zone. Clearly a ball.

He lets the call stand.

Now Capone winds up again. This time it's a curveball. I watch it spin and then sink. A fantastic pitch, but my arms know what to do. I whack the ball with a solid crack and explode down the field. My legs pump. The ball sails higher and higher. Gonna make it to second base, guaranteed.

Then I hear the sound of a distant crash. The splinter of broken glass.

I keep running, my eyes scanning the yard for the ball.

Everyone stops. They stare back at the cell house.

A cheer goes up all across the prison yard.

I broke the cell-house window.

29. STOLEN LAUNDRY

■■■■■■■■■■■■■■■■■■■■■■■■■■■■■■■

Sunday, June 7, 1936

I'm standing behind the dugout when Officer Bomini appears.

"Come with me. Keep your mouth shut. Let me do the talking," he tells me under his breath.

I follow Bomini as he lumbers toward the steep stone stairway.

On the way up the stairs, I glance back down at the baseball diamond. Capone is strutting around the pitching bag like he's emperor of baseball. The guard with the square head has his eye on me.

At the top of the stairs, Officer Bomini whistles, and an officer puts the key in the lock and swings open the heavy door. We walk back into the sweltering stillness of the cell house.

Convicts in the upper cells stare down at us as we walk down Broadway. Then I see a familiar green. My heart shoots up my chest, and my knees buckle.

Natalie.

I try to breathe. Try to think over the roar of fear.

And then slowly the scene sinks in. It's not Natalie. It's only her dress.

A convict with dark slick-backed hair is wearing the dress. He cootchy-coos his shoulders and strikes a girly pose, his feet half in Bea's old green high heels.

"Get that thing off, 292," Bomini barks.

"Somebody's always stealing from the laundry," Bomini tells me, shaking his head.

My face is clammy. I try to breathe, but my lungs are like two flat tires. This didn't come from the laundry. We left the dress and shoes in the pantry. Somebody found them.

Bomini gives me a sidelong look. "Hold yourself together, son."

We keep walking.

I listen to the echo of my footsteps on the shiny floor as we make our way down Broadway. It smells of cleaning fluid, sewage, cigarette smoke, and warm barf.

"Do not open your mouth. You understand?" Bomini's voice is barely audible. He whistles again, and the control-room officer unlocks the first barred door.

When we get to the sally port, the officer returns to the control room. Bomini leans over to consult with him. They go back and forth, Bomini angling his chin forward. He's not supposed to take a con out of here today, either.

Bomini is risking a lot for me. Fastball did, too.

My ears are trained on the whir of the electric fan, the ring of a distant phone, and the murmur of conversation.

Will they send me back?

Then a tap on the window. The officer rings us through.

I'm breathing in small bursts as I follow Bomini through the iron maiden and out the door.

On the road headed down, Bomini starts talking again,

his voice low and urgent. "You're going to walk with me down to my place. Then you're going to change your clothes. Moose? You following?"

My feet feel light, as if they're lifting off the ground. "Yes, sir," I mumble.

Up in the sky, birds fly in a sloppy line. In the bay, a buoy gently rides the water. Across the way, San Francisco shines like a brand-new baseball field.

"Keep your head down, son," Bomini barks, his blue eyes as intense as Annie's. "Gonna get complicated if you're recognized. Like I told Piper when she asked me to help you, I do not like doing this. Course I want your dad, but it's not my business who will be or won't be the warden, you understand?"

We take a hard right at the switchback and walk toward the parade grounds, then cut down the stairs to 64. Officer Bomini turns to me. "It's Bea I'd like to thrash. She thinks Darby's third in line." He snorts. "Have to get rid of all the officers and half the fish in the sea before anyone would consider him. Sticking Natalie in there . . ." His nostrils flare. "Reprehensible."

"Is Natalie okay, sir?" My voice cracks.

He nods. "Looks that way. She's sacked out at your place."

I'm shaking as I put on Bo Bomini's too-big jeans in the Bominis' bathroom and then walk outside and down the stairs to #2E, where Natalie is curled up under her purple blanket. It's too hot for covers, but Natalie doesn't care.

"You okay, Nat?" I ask.

She pulls the blanket more tightly around herself. "Home, Nat home."

I run my cut under cold water; then I walk from room to room like I've never seen the place before. The worn cushions on the sofa. The wobbly kitchen table with the folded-up cardboard under one leg. The floor lamp with the dented shade. The blue sugar and flour canisters. The icebox. My parents' dresser, missing the bottom knob. Natalie's button box, her drawing paper. The banners on my wall, the bedside table with my initials carved in the drawer. My first baseball, unstitched and flapping open on one side. And the one in my drawer, signed by the Babe and Al Capone.

30. THIS IS HER HOME

■■■■■■■■■■■■■■■■■■■■■■■■■■■■■■

Monday, June 8, 1936

When I wake up the next morning, the hall is flooded with light and the air smells of toast and peanut butter. My father is standing over me, wearing a starched white shirt with a blue tie.

This is not what the assistant warden wears to work. It's what the warden wears.

"Time to get up," he says.

I scooch up in bed. "They decided?"

He nods.

"You?"

He nods again.

I grin. "Congratulations."

"Thank you." He smiles. "They thought it was time for a change. It's a big challenge, but I think I can handle it."

"I'm proud of you, Dad."

"That means a lot to me, Moose. It's been quite the ride, I'll tell you. Yesterday was the strangest day ever."

My heart starts to beat faster. "Why?"

Dad rubs his neck. "Well, for starters, one prisoner made his own wedding gown, the priest lost his robe"—he ticks these off on his fingers—"a baseball broke the cell-house window. And then, hundreds of gulls swarmed the rec yard."

"Did you ask the priest what happened?" My voice squeaks.

Dad strokes his bald spot. "He said he didn't know, but if there's one thing men of the cloth do well, it's keep their mouths shut. A murderer can confess to a priest and he won't say boo about it."

"What about Bug?"

"Bug?"

"The black kitten that was hanging around the warden's house."

"Don't know. Haven't seen her. Why?"

My gut twists. "But Fastball's okay, right?"

He nods.

I take a deep breath. . . . "Look, I've got something to tell you," I say.

If only I could be a better brother. If only I could protect Natalie. If only I could make it all work out. My father's the warden now. Won't that make everything all right?

I pant like I've been running, cross my arms, and try to hold myself together. "Natalie ... I can't—I just can't"— I wheeze—"keep her safe here. There are too many ways she can—too many close calls." I swallow hard. "If you're the warden, she's even more of a target."

"Of course I've taken that into consideration." He chomps thoughtfully on his toothpick. "Your mother and I have talked about it. We've weighed the risk against the increase in salary, which she is going to need—"

"Dad ..."

He stops chewing.

My throat is constricted; the words come out in a croak. "Natalie was in the cell house."

His face turns white. His teeth splinter the toothpick in two. "She was not."

"She was."

"I would have known."

I shake my head.

"Did anything . . . happen?"

"I don't think so."

"You don't *think* so?"

Tears well up in my chest. "I did the best I could—"

He shakes his head. "This can't be true."

"Bea told her to go in. She hid her in one of those giant soup pots. She wanted to cause trouble so you wouldn't get the promotion . . . and Darby would."

He shakes his head harder. "Not even Bea would do that."

"She did. She's awful. You have to get rid of her."

"Who told you this?"

"Piper told me Nat was in the cell house. You were off the island with the BOP men. There wasn't time to get you. . . ."

My father's hand trembles as he searches for a toothpick in his pocket.

"Everybody says I look like the Nose. All I could think of was to put on your old uniform and pretend I was him."

"You walked right in?" His voice is sharp.

"I found her hidden in the kitchen. Fastball was keeping an eye on her. I know I'm not supposed to trust any con, but—"

My father nods. "I'd trust Fastball more than the rest of them."

"Yeah, Fastball helped. But Fang had a shiv." I show him the cut mark on my arm.

"Oh." He gulps. "When we're done, you go on up to Doc Ollie's and have him see if that needs stitches."

"I'm fine. Look, it wasn't me Fang wanted. It was Natalie. He almost got her."

His legs give way. He sits down with a thump.

I go on. "People saw us. But nobody wanted me or Natalie to get found out. Nose and Mr. Bomini helped, too. Most of the cons want you to be the warden. So do the Mattamans."

He grinds his jaw. I hear the crack. "How'd you get out?"

"Nat wore the priest's robe. Bomini got me out dressed in convict clothes. Listen, Dad. Nat brought your gun to the ballpark. She heard Scout telling me I should bring something really spectacular and I could get on the team. He suggested a gun. He was just kidding. Natalie took it literally."

"Natalie brought the gun?"

I sigh. "I knew it would be worse if it was her."

His eyelids twitch.

"You took the blame?"

I nod. "Dad, she can't live here if you're the warden."

"This is her home, Moose." His lip trembles. "I'm not going to tell my own daughter she can't come home."

"What if I'm not around one day? What if you aren't? The warden's house is right next to the cell house."

"But your mother . . ."

"She can't handle this anymore. Can't you see that?"

He flinches like I just poked him hard. "My girls." His voice trembles.

His eyes focus on a baseball banner on my wall. They are looking through it to some middle space.

When he finally looks back at me, he says: "I've put you in an impossible situation." His voice breaks. "You shouldn't be the one to have to handle all this."

His words fill up a hole inside me.

"What are we going to do now?" he asks, though the question doesn't seem directed at me.

"Carrie Kelly is helping her more than we are," I say. My voice breaks.

He pulls out his handkerchief and blows his nose. His eyelids are rimmed in red. He presses his hands together. His chin leans against his fingertips. His eyes are somewhere else.

He sits like this for a long time. When he finally opens his mouth, he says: "Never thought you'd be the one to tell me this. But now that you've said it, I don't know why I didn't see it before."

31. MRS. PASSERINI

....

Thursday, June 11, 1936

My mom, my dad, and Carrie Kelly have long meetings about Natalie. Carrie Kelly likes the idea of Natalie living part-time with her and part-time at the Esther P. Marinoff. She thinks Natalie is ready for more independence.

Mrs. Kelly got Nat a job working in the accounting department of her school one afternoon a week. She's started a social-skills class with some of the other students. Things are going better than even Mrs. Kelly dared to hope. Though everyone is concerned about Natalie's obsession with Passerini. Mrs. Kelly told my parents we need to deal with this.

How do you get Natalie to understand that Passerini was just being nice—he doesn't want to marry her? How do you explain that I only said she could marry him to get her to cooperate in the cell house?

My mother told her she's too young to get married, and besides, it wasn't a real ring. My father said he wouldn't allow it. But none of this has made any difference to Natalie.

"Mrs. Passerini. Moose said," Nat tells them, like I'm the final word on everything.

"You told her that?" My father stares at me.

"What choice did I have?"

"That was when you were trying to get her to put on the uniform?"

"Yes."

"Oh," my mother groans. She closes her eyes and massages her temple. "Could you just have your friend tell her he doesn't want to marry her?"

"It's not that easy, Mom."

My father catches my mother's eye. He cocks his head toward me.

"Nothing about this is easy," my mom agrees. She takes an awkward step in my direction. When she gets close, she wraps her arms around me as if she's just remembered how to do this.

"I am so sorry, Moose. I should have known you wouldn't take Dad's gun. I can't believe we punished you for that. Shame on us. You have always, *always* had Natalie's best interests in mind. Sometimes"—she rubs her eyes—"I let my worry about Natalie get the best of me. I get so wrapped up in it, I can't see anything else."

"Yeah, I've noticed," I say.

She sits down hard. "We career from one crisis to another, and I lose sight of . . . of what it must be like to be you." She looks up at me.

My father nods. "We aren't going to do that anymore. And I won't send you and Natalie in to deal with this Passerini situation alone. We'll sort it out together."

No . . . oh no! I can just imagine my parents showing up at practice, trying to explain everything to Passerini. It's bad enough that Natalie's there.

I back away so fast, I bump into the coffee table. "That's okay, Dad."

My father lets out a surprised laugh. "He doesn't want us, Helen."

"Apparently not," Mom says.

"Look, I'm the one that promised her," I mumble. "I'll figure it out."

Back in my room, I pack the signed baseball in my bag. Capone said not to take it, but anyone who wants Trixle to be warden has to be cracked. Besides, Capone doesn't have a sister like Natalie. He doesn't know how hard this is. He won't know what I do with the baseball anyway. He doesn't have eyes everywhere. He's not as powerful as he thinks he is.

Last night, the fog poured in, and the foghorn began booming low and tubalike. Better this than the blistering heat, so long as the ferry is running, and it is.

Scout said we'd meet at the park, so Nat and I go straight there from Fort Mason. Nat has on a new skirt and blouse Mom got for her. It isn't like her old dresses. And it isn't like the two Bea Trixle gave her. She looks nice.

Even so, I'm hoping Passerini won't show up. But when we arrive, he's already there, leaning against the bleachers in his white shirt and shoes with no socks. He looks up from lacing his glove. "Hi."

Natalie flaps her fingers down low in the folds of her skirt. "Passerini," she mutters.

Passerini's smile looks uncomfortable.

"Hey, Pass, Passerini, look." Her eyes glow as she shows him the button ring bobbling on her hand.

"Oh." His eyes dart to me.

"I want to marry you," Nat says.

My knees wobble. My face gets hot. Scout runs up, then stops a few feet away, watching.

"Well . . ." Passerini's eyes skitter and then settle. He takes a deep breath. "I'd like to, but I share a room with my little brother."

I stand behind Nat and nod at Pass. He keeps going. "You can't get married when you share a room. You probably already know that."

Nat shakes her head, her mouth twitching.

"It's a rule," I add, continuing to nod my encouragement to Passerini.

"That's right." Passerini's voice is more confident now. "It's a rule at my house."

"A rule at my house," Nat echoes.

"It's a rule at everybody's house," I add. "Scout, is it a rule at your house?"

"Yes, it is," Scout says.

Nat wrinkles her nose. Her mouth stretches in different directions. She stands stock-still, looking down at her feet, then walks back to the bleachers. She sits with her hands wedged deeply under her legs and stays that way for a long time.

When Beck arrives, he comes straight over. "I understand you got the photo?"

I frown at Scout.

"That's what you said on the phone. You said you had something big," Scout says.

I turn and face Beck. "I don't."

Beck cocks his head. "Too bad. Would have been nice to have you."

Scout leaps forward. "You said you had something, Moose. You said I wouldn't believe it until I saw it with my own eyes!"

"Nope," I tell Scout.

"Moose, come on," Scout says. "You know you did."

I look Beck straight in his shrewd little eyes. "We're either good enough for your team or we're not."

"That's easy." Beck juts his chin out. "You're not."

"Moose." Scout fixes me with two pleading eyeballs.

I stand up straight and step forward until I'm up close to Beck's face. I lock my knees to stop them from shaking. "You've played with us."

"Yeah, so?"

"That day you played against Southy. If we were on your team, you wouldn't have lost."

"Right," he snorts, rolling his eyes. "Look, there are a lot of guys who want to be on this team, and they aren't freshmen."

"Ask your team if they want us."

"*I'm* the captain. I decide."

"Okay then." I shrug. "Scout, let's go." I turn around and start walking away.

"Moose," Scout hisses. "Don't be crazy."

"Just keep walking," I say under my breath.

Scout stays with me, but he's dragging his feet and grumbling. We just get past the bleachers when Dewey comes running up.

"One-month trial." He pants.

"Great." Scout gently punches my arm.

"No, not great," I say. "What happens then?"

"Beck decides," Dewey says.

"No," I say.

"No?" Scout stares at me.

I level my eyes at Dewey. "At the end of the month, the team votes us in or out."

Dewey looks from me to Scout, then runs back to Beck with the message.

Scout stares like I've grown a third arm. We watch Dewey make his way back to us.

"He said okay," Dewey pants. He smiles at us.

Scout grins. We all nod; then Scout and I walk back to Natalie.

Scout shakes his head. "I can't believe you did that."

I shrug, kicking my baseball bat with my toe. "A little something I learned from Al Capone."

■ ■

Thursday, June 11, 1936

We don't exactly know which ferry Fastball will get on, on account of we're not supposed to be on the dock when prisoners are transported. But half of 64 Building is here fishing for cappazoni or checking crab pots down on the rocks or eating ice cream or waiting in line for the phone.

A man taking his first free steps isn't a sight you see every day. Nobody wants to miss it.

I sit with my legs dangling over the side of the dock, my heels kicking the washed-out lines that mark the water levels. The water rises and falls under the wooden slats. The rowboat tugs against its mooring. The buoy bell *ding-ding-ding*s.

What's it feel like to walk out of prison? Where do you go? How do you get money? How do you convince a landlord to take a chance on you? How do you get a job when so many men who haven't committed crimes are out of work?

Piper sits down next to me. She's wearing her old overalls. "Hi," she says.

"Hi." I kick the piling. My shoe flaps off. I lean down to slip it back on.

"So," she says. "My dad's retiring."

"I heard."

We listen to the wind lash the tattered flag. "I'll miss this place, but at least I don't have to go back to boarding school. My mom thinks I won't get into trouble if we don't live on a prison island."

"Is that true?" I ask.

She shrugs.

I stare into the lapping water. "Thank you for telling me what Bea did and for sending Mr. Bomini to get me."

"Pretty amazing you went in after her. I never thought you'd do that."

"What was I supposed to do?"

"You could have done a lot of other things." She fixes her eyes on me. "It was brave. Hey, you've forgiven me about the gun, right? Natalie said you would. She even made a new rule. *Always forgive your friends.*"

"She did or you did?"

Piper pulls a splintered piece of wood off the dock. "Might have been both of us."

I pull off another piece and hand it to her. "Hey, I've been wondering . . . did the prisoners get to Bug?"

Piper's face darkens. "I haven't seen her."

"At all?"

Piper shakes her head. "Nope."

I look out at the deep blue water and try not to think about Fang's big, murdering hands.

"I was supposed to watch her. I told Fastball I would." I kick the piling so hard my heel hurts.

I want her to say it wasn't my fault. Instead, she asks: "Where's Natalie?"

"Getting ready to go. Hey, wait ... what ever happened with your dad?"

She wobbles her head. "He says I have to earn his respect, and I'm not exactly there yet." She sighs. "He'll be easier to get along with when he isn't the warden anymore. It's a lot of pressure. I hope your dad can handle it."

"Yeah, me too." I look up at a lone gull with gray-tipped wings flying in the middle sky.

"Are you going to move into my room?"

"How should I know? Probably spend most of my time in 64 Building."

"You practically live at the Mattamans' anyway. . . ." She takes out a pack of gum and offers me one. "So, do you forgive me or not . . . ?"

I shrug.

"I had to tell my dad about the gun. I had to."

I take a good, hard look at her. "You could have kept your mouth shut. But you know what made me the maddest? That *we* were in the wrong. My father shouldn't have had his gun at home, and Nat shouldn't have taken it."

She grins. "I liked that part, too. Though, to be fair, it wasn't your fault."

"I've never known you to be fair."

"Yeah, well . . . that's new." She threads her fingers through her hair. "When's Annie coming home?"

"I don't know."

"Probably be home early. She can't stay away from you, you know."

"We're just friends now, Annie and me."

Piper rolls her eyes. "In your mind, Moose Flanagan, not in hers."

I swing my legs over the water. "That's not true."

She shakes her head, her lips bunched to one side. "Nobody gets over you."

"What's that supposed to mean?" I ask as the phone outside 64 Building rings. Mrs. Mattaman answers it.

"It means people like you, okay?"

"People?"

"Yeah, people."

Mrs. Mattaman waves her arm to Theresa and Jimmy.

Theresa scrambles up from the rocks and runs over to her mother. "He's coming!" she shouts.

Jimmy drops his crab trap back in the water and climbs up to us.

We look up the switchback, to where my dad and Fastball are walking down.

Fastball doesn't look right in civilian clothes. His hat sits too high on his head. His sport jacket is a size too small. His pass man uniform was always a good fit.

Normally when a guard transports a prisoner, the prisoner is cuffed to the guard. But my father and Fastball are walking side by side like friends. I guess there aren't rules for how a prisoner is discharged from Alcatraz on account of it hasn't happened before.

We watch them make their way down the hill. We aren't supposed to be on the dock, so we can't exactly yell "Bye, Fastball." And of course we can't shake his hand. I can't look him in the eye anyway, on account of Bug.

But each of us has a gift for him. Jimmy and me gave him our game, Escape from Alcatraz, which we changed so there's a way you can win by getting released. Natalie and me got him a baseball. Not the signed one, of course; the kind you play with every day. Theresa gave him her entire savings: two dollars and eleven cents. Piper and Natalie made him a little book.

How to Be Free, by Natalie Flanagan
(With help from Piper Williams)

1. *If you get angry, lie on your hands.*
2. *If you're confused, count stuff.*
3. *If you want to start your day over, flip the light switch.*
4. *It's hard to make friends. Keep trying.*
5. *Don't give up on people. Everybody messes up now and then.*
6. *Don't forget to watch the sunrise.*
7. *You can be as happy as the people in magazines.*
8. *Stick by your brother. Nobody will ever love you as much as he does.*

These are pretty good rules. I'm impressed.

If I were to write my own, I wonder what I'd come up with? Maybe something like:

Work hard, play fair, stand up for yourself, and don't let anything happen to any kittens.

We put our gifts in a flour sack. Theresa has them now. She dashes to the ferry berth, drops the bag behind Fastball, and then runs back to us.

But the bag moves. Wait . . . it couldn't have. Then it moves again. A paw sticks out.

"Bug." My voice cracks.

Jimmy looks over at me, his eyes wide. "Theresa hid him in our apartment. Didn't you know that?"

I shake my head, so relieved, it feels like a ball and chain have been removed from my leg. "Man, do I owe her for that."

Jimmy nods. "Theresa's not bad, you know, for a sister."

My father turns around and scoops up the bag just as Bug's head pokes out. He shakes her back inside and hands the bag to Fastball.

Fastball lifts the kitten out. Bug's paws go up around Fastball's neck.

Fastball flashes a smile warm enough to burn the fog off our entire island. He wipes his face with his shaky hand, holds Bug close, and starts walking again.

My father follows him onto the ferry. Then my mother and Natalie get on. Natalie is wearing a new striped dress and carrying her suitcase. She looks like a young woman someone might hire for a bookkeeping job.

Nat's used to staying at the Esther P. Marinoff, so being off the island is part of her normal routine. Now, when she's not at school, she'll stay with Carrie Kelly and eventually maybe in a rooming house with other young women her age. Hard to know how that will turn out.

I'm not sure what was decided about how often she'll

come home. It won't be never, but it will be a lot less. Most of the time, we'll visit her at Carrie Kelly's. This will be an adjustment, but it's important. We all know that. It's not safe for her here.

Fastball stops and surveys the seats like he can't decide which one to take. In the cell house, you don't get to choose where you sit. You don't get to choose anything.

Fastball glances back at my father. My father's hands open like he doesn't know. Bug is perched on Fastball's shoulder. Petting her seems to steady him. After a long minute, he picks a seat.

Natalie doesn't have this problem. She knows exactly what she wants.

Fastball gives us one long look, tips his hat, and then turns his eyes to the city across the way.

"Bye, Fastball! Bye, Natalie!" Theresa can't stop herself from waving. She's got both arms going.

And then we all wave. Every one of us. Even the adults.

It's Jimmy who starts the clapping. We give a standing ovation to Natalie and Fastball as the *Coxe* pulls out, carving a wide white wake in the deep blue water.

Fastball waves back, but Natalie doesn't. Her finger moves methodically from person to person, counting us. We are her family. We'll be the count she holds on to wherever she goes.

I keep waving until the ferry is small enough to fit in my pocket. And then I let her go.

ACKNOWLEDGMENTS

■ ■

First, I'd like to thank my agent, Elizabeth Harding. Without her help shepherding this manuscript, it would still be stuck in the hard drive between my ears.

Thanks to Wendy Lamb and her esteemed team: Dana Carey, Eryn Levine, Grace Weatherall, Elizabeth Stranahan, Elena Meuse, Katharine Cooper, and Colleen Fellingham for helping me to write the very best book I could. Dana Carey's expert sleuthing located information that was pivotal to the plot of this book. Wendy Lamb saw a glimmer of what I wanted to do and wouldn't give up until I turned that book in. I will always be grateful to her for that.

A big thank-you to Peter Seraichick, my baseball consultant, and to the rangers and volunteers on Alcatraz, especially John Cantwell and Lori Brosnan. Lori was my boss all those many years ago when I volunteered on Alcatraz. John and Lori were responsible for most of the alumni days I attended (1998 to 2017). Those days were so helpful to me. A special thank-you to Chuck Stucker, George DeVincenzi, Robert Luke, Jolene Babyak, Phyllis Twinney, and everyone in the Alcatraz alumni family. And thank you to Michael Esslinger, whose book on Alcatraz is always my go-to source, and Dick

Miner, whose *Al Capone Does My Shirts* garden tour of Alcatraz is extremely popular with fourth-, fifth-, and sixth-grade classes. All these people were sources of information who have now become friends. Who knew a prison could attract such lovely people?

AUTHOR'S NOTE

■ ■

Al Capone on Alcatraz

Al Capone was an inmate on Alcatraz Island from August 22, 1934, to January 6, 1939. I chose to set the series in 1935 and 1936 because I thought he would make a compelling character. I was intrigued by descriptions of him making appearances in Chicago wearing diamond pinkie rings, and overcoats in extravagant colors with the right-handed pocket made larger and stronger to fit his gun. His silk underwear budget may have been as much as $5,000[1] a year (approximately $70,000 today).

Mostly, he was a terrible man—a ruthless mob boss who employed a staff of seven hundred gunmen and controlled much of Chicago. "He told the police of America's second largest city what to do, and the police obeyed."[2]

Not surprisingly, Capone's behavior did not change once he went to prison. He tried to secure preferential treatment

---

[1] Jonathan Eig, *Get Capone: The Secret Plot That Captured America's Most Wanted Gangster* (New York: Simon & Schuster, 2010), 294.

[2] John Kobler, *Capone: The Life and World of Al Capone* (New York: G.P. Putnam's Sons, 1971), 16.

through bribery and extortion. Before being sent to Alcatraz, he was remarkably successful. He managed to use jail... "as the new headquarters for his criminal enterprise ... he had the freedom to make phone calls, send telegrams, and dispatch messengers around the city. He even had secretarial help.... when guests arrived, Capone served them good whiskey."

Capone was incarcerated in Eastern State Penitentiary in 1929.
The prison re-created his cell.

"On Thanksgiving, the prisoner [Capone] was permitted to skip the prison fare and sup from a huge hamper of food sent by his mother ... after the meal, an ice-cream truck pulled up outside the jail and delivered a slice of layer cake and a scoop of ice cream to each prisoner in the facility, compliments of inmate Capone."[3]

---

[3] Eig, *Get Capone,* 370.

Capone was sent to Alcatraz because of his previously pampered existence behind bars and to garner publicity for the new prison. The Great Depression was debilitating and crime was rampant. The maximum-security prison on Alcatraz was a symbol of the terrible fate that would befall you if you pursued a life of crime. J. Edgar Hoover knew the most effective way to get that message across was to send America's best-known criminal to do time there.

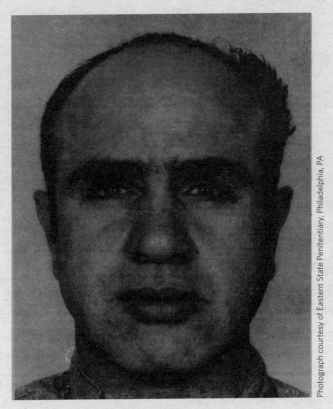

Photograph courtesy of Eastern State Penitentiary, Philadelphia, PA

Al Capone's mug shot.

The first thing Capone did after arriving on Alcatraz was to attempt to persuade Warden James A. Johnston to extend special privileges to him. "[Capone] was suave and aggressive by turns, and it was apparent from the beginning that he was trying to show the other prisoners that he would find some way to get what he wanted inside, just as he had always got what he wanted when he was outside."[4]

On Alcatraz, Capone secured no special treatment except perhaps better medical care. Capone was the warden's "star boarder."[5] If something happened to him, it would bring negative publicity to the prison.

Al Capone's cell on Alcatraz.

---

[4] James A. Johnston, *Alcatraz Island Prison and the Men Who Live There*. (Douglas/Ryan Communication, 1999), 40.

[5] Johnston, *Alcatraz Island Prison*, 30.

All Al Capone dialogue was invented. But the quote from Babe Ruth on page 84 is real.[6]

Al Capone and Baseball

In addition to being an accomplished criminal, Capone loved baseball. During his Chicago years, he was often seen watching games from expensive box seats. As a boy he "pitched sandlot baseball well enough to cherish dreams of turning pro."[7] In his thirties he aspired to buy the Chicago Cubs and Wrigley Field.[8]

Sources differ on whether Capone played baseball on Alcatraz. One former inmate claimed: "Capone used to play and tried to run the team, but he made so many errors on first they put him on the field. Al's feelings were hurt, and he stamped his foot and cursed the fellows. If he couldn't play first base and manage the team, he wouldn't play at all."[9]

A member of my ace editorial team, Dana Carey, discovered the baseball signed by Al Capone and Babe Ruth. The baseball, believed to be authentic, was apparently, signed by Capone at Comiskey Park in 1931. The pitcher, Herb

[6]   Babe Ruth, William R. Cobb, and Paul Dickson, *Playing the Game: My Early Years in Baseball* (Mineola, NY: Dover Publications, 2011), 27.

[7]   Robert J. Schoenberg, *Mr. Capone: The Real—and Complete—Story of Al Capone* (New York: Morrow, 1992), 21.

[8]   Deirdre Marie Capone, *Uncle Al Capone* (Bonita Springs, FL: Recap Publishing Company, 2011), 45.

[9]   Al Best [pseud.], "Inside Alcatraz: The Prison Memories of Inmate Number 107: The Untold Story of Al Capone on the Rock," ed. Richard Reinhardt, *San Francisco Focus,* December 1987, 130.

Pennock, had approached Capone, who signed the ball and gave it back. Later, Herb got his teammate Babe Ruth to sign the same ball.[10] It was auctioned on eBay in 2013 for $62,000.[11]

Capone/Ruth baseball.

Photograph courtesy of Mile High Card Company

It wasn't just Capone who loved baseball. Most everybody on Alcatraz did. During the later years of its operation, the prison's game scores were posted next to the major league game scores on the cell house menu board every morning.

Kids on Alcatraz

Kids lived on Alcatraz Island because their fathers were guards. "64 Building was not only home for approximately

---

[10] Neil Hayes, "The Hero and the Bad Guy," *New York Daily News,* http://www.milehighcardco.com/UserFiles/image/nydailynewsarticle.jpg.

[11] "Ruth-Capone Signed Baseball Auctions Online for $62,000," on JustCollecting website, accessed May 23, 2017, https://www.justcollecting .com/miscellania/ruth-capone-signed-baseball-auctions-online-for-62-000.

Photograph courtesy of the National Park Service, GGNRA, Betty Wallar Collection

Cons playing baseball on Alcatraz.

twenty-five families, but also housed a well-stocked market called 'the canteen.'"[12]

In the event of an emergency, the warden needed his men to be close at hand. The dangers of women and children on a maximum-security prison island were outweighed by the convenience and low cost of Alcatraz accommodations.

Kids living on the island sometimes had contact with convicts. The convicts did the laundry and picked up the trash. They were gardeners and handymen, plumbers, painters, and electricians. They frequently worked on the dock directly in front of 64 Building. The kids got used to seeing them and vice versa.

---

[12] Hurley, Donald J., *Alcatraz Island Memories* (Sonoma, CA: Fog Bell Enterprises, 1987), 61.

As Florence Madigan, the daughter of Warden Madigan, put it: "They [the convicts] all knew who all of us were." Patrick Mahoney said: "Once I passed a candy bar through a fence to a convict on a work crew. . . . We weren't supposed to, but we played near the fence within earshot of the prisoners and frequently talked to the convicts."[13]

As a child, living on Alcatraz gave you bragging rights at school in San Francisco. Some children even found ways to monetize their unique digs. "I invented my own job at school," explained Mahoney. "I signed people up to come to the island on Saturdays and sometimes Sundays as well. The trip cost a dollar. I'd pick up my 'guest' at Fort Mason's pier #2 waiting room and send him or her back in the next boat, an hour later. On a typical Saturday, I had as many as ten 'guests' . . . I would leave their names and the time of their visit with the guard at the entry to Lower Fort Mason."[14]

Kids did take the ferry back and forth to school. And in the early penitentiary years, the ferry would sometimes be grounded because of intense fog. This was known as a Fog Day.

Pass men worked in the warden's house. The cook and the houseboy were generally convicts, though the character Fastball is completely fictional. But the rule that convicts could under no circumstances touch a child is factual. As

---

[13] Patrick Mahoney, *Assignment Alcatraz: My Dirty, Wonderful Job* (San Francisco: Golden Gate National Parks Conservancy, 2013), 124.

[14] Mahoney, *Assignment Alcatraz*, 131.

Ferry schedule.

Florence Madigan explained, "One day I was taking garbage out and fell down the steps. The pass man saw me fall and came running to pick me up. The pass man could have lost his job for being kind."[15]

There is no record of kids sneaking into the main part of the cell house, although the huge soup pots would have made a great hiding place. There are no known cases of escapes or

---

[15] Florence Madigan, speech on Alcatraz Island for Alcatraz Alumni Day, August 2014.

attempted escapes in a priest's robes—at least, not on Alcatraz. The idea for that scene came from an attempted escape
at San Quentin State Prison.

Soup pot.

Prison Life

It's true that inmates were almost never paroled directly from
Alcatraz. The rule of silence was also a fact of the early Alcatraz penitentiary years, and it was terribly unpopular. In July
of 1935, the *San Francisco Examiner* ran a headline article
entitled "Alcatraz Silence Awful."

The rule that prohibited convicts from communicating
to one another was one of the complaints that launched the
prisoner strike of 1936, though the strike happened in January, not May, as in this book. "In January of 1936, nearly one

hundred and forty inmates went on strike to protest the rule of silence and the lack of privileges at Alcatraz."[16] I fictionalized other aspects of the strike as well.

Al Capone was not the mastermind of any strikes. In fact, "Al Capone did not go on strike. Kelly, Bates, and Bailey, the Oklahoma kidnappers, advised him not to have a thing to do with it. If he did, the officials would accuse him of being the leader."[17]

There was a shooting range on the island, and the guards were expected to practice marksmanship. The warden reported to the Bureau of Prisons; however, it is highly unlikely that a man like Cam Flanagan with eighteen months' experience would be asked to run the prison.

Natalie

Growing up is difficult for everybody, but it can be especially challenging for teens on the autism spectrum. My older sister, Gina Johnson, had classic autism. Though most of Natalie's story is fictional, the spirit of the battle Gina fought to become an adult informs my words. It is my hope that we can all be as gracious and kind as Moose and Passerini when we come into contact with teens on the spectrum struggling to find a place in the world.

---

[16] Michael Esslinger, *Alcatraz: A Definitive History of the Penitentiary Years* (Carmel, CA: Ocean View Publishing, 2003), 133.

[17] Best, *Inside Alcatraz,* 128.

"Help these walls come tumbling down…"

Gina Johnson, at age eight, and without speech, drew this picture of herself inside the wall which surrounds her and many other children like her, showing her recognition of her terrible predicament in life. Let us help bring these walls tumbling down.

Photograph courtesy of the author

Gennifer's sister, Gina.

Read all the exciting Tales from Alcatraz!

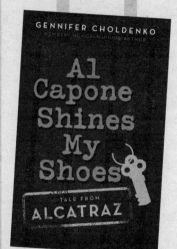

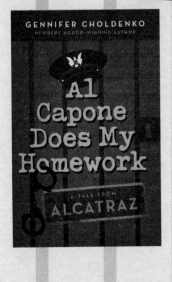

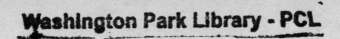